CRASH COURSE

CRASH COURSE

TANIS BROWNING-SHELP

DOG-EARED BOOKS

This book is published by Dog-Eared Books, Ottawa, Ontario.
www.dog-earedbooks.com

Editors: Jennifer Latham and Linda Poitevin
Cover Art: Jocelyn van Wynsberghe
Author Photograph: Helene Anne Fortin
Production and Design: Jen Hamilton

Library and Archives Canada Cataloguing in Publication

Browning-Shelp, Tanis, 1964-, author
    Crash course / Tanis Browning-Shelp.

ISBN 978-0-9953360-1-8 (softcover)

    I. Title.

PS8603.R698C73 2016   jC813'.6   C2016-907580-X

To my friends and family, for believing

TABLE OF CONTENTS

SEASON OPENER

Maryn O'Brien's heart pounded in her head like a hammer against her helmet. She grunted with the force of shoving her feet against the pedals. Her breath came out in gasps. At two kilometres into the race, she was well ahead of the pack, but her forearms ached and her grip on the mountain bike's handlebars weakened. She'd gone out too fast. Too hard.

She focused on the trail ahead. The course had lots of tight turns and steep rocky parts. She knew each rise, twist, and drop as well as she knew her own pencil-case doodles. But if she didn't pay attention, she could still get smacked by a low-hanging branch or knocked around by loose stones. The morning's light rain had added another layer of fun—slick rocks and muck that pulled at her wheels like zombie hands.

"Come on, Maryn, step up your game!" she hissed between huffs.

Starting too hard in a race was such a rookie mistake—often ending in hyperventilating or hurling—and with six years of training and racing under her belt, she was no rookie.

She willed herself to slow down, struggling to control her breathing. Banking sharp left into the trees, she snuck a peek over her shoulder. No Emma Sutcliffe. Darn it! The fact that her archrival and most serious challenger was nowhere to be seen proved Maryn had gotten carried away in the excitement of the season's first race. No novice herself, Emma had obviously been smarter about pacing herself at the start. Maryn pushed away the panic stirring in her chest. She still had the advantage of being familiar with the course. Thank god her own team, the Radical Off-Roadies, was hosting the Ontario Cup season opener and that they trained on these trails almost every day of the week. Racing on home turf definitely meant she could—and should—beat Emma Sutcliffe. But only if she got herself under control.

Maryn sucked in deep breaths of the pine-scented air. Calm and strength returned, bringing focus with them. She pumped her legs steadily, her sharp gaze taking in the small patches of ice along the edges of the track in the cool shade of the towering pines. Nature may have cooperated by ending the early May rain in time for the race, but bikers still needed to have respect for it. An ice patch concealed by leaves could cause an ugly crash, taking an unwary athlete out of the race—and maybe even out of the season.

She burst out of the trees and spun past the spectators lined up along a fence at the edge of the clubhouse parking lot. She took in the banner draped above the clubhouse door. In huge red letters, it shouted out "Home of the Radical Off-Roadies racing team!"

A man wearing her team's signature red tee ran along the barrier, keeping pace with her.

"That's right, Maryn. Breath and spin...breath and spin," Coach Webber yelled, clapping his hands to punctuate his words. "Now don't ramp it up again until the fork at the eight-kilometre mark!"

She flew along the open stretch for about fifty metres, then spotted her parents, Fuller and Darby O'Brien, her brother Gil, and her best friend, Janey Cunningham. Her dad hollered with the same crazed enthusiasm he'd shown ever since she'd tackled her first trail ride with him at age four. "That's right, Sprint! *You* show 'em who owns these trails!"

Despite her burning lungs, she grinned. *Dad gets so hyped when I race!*

Her mom took a more collected approach. "Way to stay strong, Maryn. Looking good," she called out as she leaned over the fence.

Maryn nodded at Mom and then flashed Janey a comforting smile. Her friend looked so stressed. Janey hated these raccs—hated competition, period. But there she was, screeching like a fiend because she was such an awesome BFF.

Maryn's wheels turned up gravel. Her brother Gil sounded an alert. "Emma just came out of the woods, Maryn. You've got twenty-five metres on her." The warning helped because it meant that Maryn didn't have to check behind her as she re-entered the forest. Looking back could cost you the race. Twenty-five metres was a big lead for sure, but Emma could close that gap.

Today, twenty-three girls competed in their category: CADET, UNDER 17, EXPERT. She and Emma often battled it out for first place, with the rest of the girls in their category being left out of contention for the gold or silver.

Maryn always chased the gold, but today, with everyone from her club cheering her on, she wanted it even more. She had her breathing under control, but her legs shook beneath her as she stood to attack a steep climb. Her wheels slid sideways under the torque of her strong pedal strokes. The mud and ice menaced. But she stayed tight on tricky corners, used her gears effectively, and rode cleanly. At the eight-kilometre mark of the 10K race, Emma's tires crunched through the terrain just a few metres back. Maryn trained her eyes forward and ramped it up at the fork just like Coach Webber said.

She pushed hard. The cracks and whooshes behind her drove her even harder. *I know this trail. I've felt this burn. I've got this!*

"ROCKY" ROCKS!

Sweat streamed down Maryn's forehead. Her eyes stung, but she took no notice. She panted to the pulse of her pedal strokes in a powerful sprint to the finish. Then she sailed across the line in first place, punching the air with her right fist.

Coach Webber greeted her a few minutes later with a high five and a huge grin. "Nice work, Maryn!"

Her joy at her win grew, deepening her confidence. Coach measured her performances against goals she set for herself. Sometimes he pointed out places where she could have raced better, even if she did win. But not today. This was just the kind of feedback she needed to help achieve her prime goal of competing in the Olympics.

"They'll be presenting the medals soon," Coach said. "They have the podium set up over by the barbecue pit. I'll see you there in a bit. I just wanna check the overall results."

Maryn's stomach fluttered. She felt like such a show-off at medal presentations. This race had been good practice, but she preferred to think of it as just another step in the right direction. She grabbed her bike from where she had leaned it against the side of the clubhouse after her cooldown. The building was a huge, one-storey prefab metal structure christened 'the Garage' by club members. She turned the corner. Oh crap! She stopped in her tracks, a bit stunned by how many people had stayed for the awards.

Her dad called out, "There she is!" and several people turned to look. Her face warmed. She tried to smooth down her massive head of sandy curls as she pushed her bike towards the crowd gathered around the makeshift podium. Her hair had expanded in the humid spring breeze after being released from its bike helmet prison. When it grew to these proportions, her brother called it her 'insano mano.'

Three wooden boxes turned upside down served as the bike club's podium. The tall box for the gold medal winner stood in the centre. These boxes doubled as the club's lost and found and ordinarily sat near the Garage's lockers, filled with random gloves, helmets, and tire pumps.

Maryn's dad strode towards her. "How did the ol' Rockhopper perform today?" he asked, squatting down to take stock of the royal blue and red Rockhopper Comp 29 mountain bike. "I tuned it up myself at the shop yesterday." He jiggled Maryn's race number plate to see if it had come loose during the race.

"It doesn't matter how many mechanics you hire at O'Brien's Bikes, does it?" Maryn laughed. "You still take matters into your own hands."

"Only where my daughter is concerned." He began to run through a check of the chain, brakes, and gears, flicking away mud with his fingers.

"Rocky handled well today," Maryn said. She and her dad always gave their bikes nicknames.

"Actually, I'd say that Rocky was well handled by *you* today," her dad said, putting his arm around Maryn's shoulders and giving her an affectionate squeeze. "Bravo, Sprint! You really gutted it out this morning."

"Thanks, Dad."

"If today's performance is any indication of the season ahead, we might have to look at replacing your humble steed," her dad remarked, just as her mom, Gil, and Janey walked up.

"You'd replace your precious Rocky?" Gil asked, with one eyebrow raised. "You spend more time with that bike than you do with your own friends." He gave Janey a wink. "Imagine how bummed a boy-friend would be about Rocky."

Janey, like Maryn, was one grade ahead of Gil. But Gil had the confidence of a high school senior, and the glint in his eyes disarmed people. He had inherited Mom's straight, jet-black hair and husky-blue eyes along with Dad's tall stature. Fourteen years old and approaching the end of grade eight, he already stood nearly six feet tall and, while he hadn't yet confided in Maryn, she'd caught wind that he had a girl-friend. Younger than Maryn by just ten months, he now towered over her. *Some 'big' sister,* she thought, pulling her five-foot-six frame up next to his, and then sagging back again in defeat.

"Boyfriend?" she scoffed, rolling her eyes. "As *if*. Not everyone feels the need to couple up, Gil."

At fifteen, Maryn was at the end of her grade nine year. She, Janey, and Gil all attended J.T. Seeley Collegiate. It drove her crazy that everyone adored her brother, and that even girls in her own grade were crushing on him. *Why can't I make friends that easily?* She glared at him, just for being Gil.

"Whoa…easy…why the dirty look?" he asked. "Shouldn't you be thanking me for coming out to cheer you on? I mean, this isn't exactly a spectator sport, you know."

"Oh, right. And baseball is? I'd rather sit around watching Janey's toenail polish dry than sit through another nine innings of watching you pitch!"

"Hey!" Janey objected. "Please leave me out of this. And, well, I hardly ever wear toenail polish."

"How can you say baseball's boring?" Gil asked. "At least we don't all just disappear into the woods for fifteen minutes at a time."

Janey turned the talk back to bikes. "Are you really gonna replace Rocky?"

"Well, Dad says if Coach gives me the thumbs up to advance from the Ontario Cup Series to doing some *Canada* Cup racing next season, he wants to upgrade my ride. But I don't know…" She trailed off, patting her bike's frame. "Rocky has been good to me."

"Rocky is in the budget category, really, but performs like a bike double its price!" Her dad's emphasis showed his fondness for the model. He had been selling that bike in his shop for years because it made for happy customers.

"Peoples' eyes are glazing over, Fuller," Mom warned.

"Oh, but this is fascinating stuff," he insisted. "You see, Janey, through twenty years of refinement, this bike now has spot-on geometry, increased leverage for precise handling…a short stem and wide handlebar."

"Dad!" Maryn interrupted. "I'm the only one who cares. Seriously, nobody has a clue what you're talking about." She turned to Janey and apologized. "You know how Dad is a really old school mountain biker, right?"

"Sure."

"Well that means he kind of speaks a different language than normal humans. It usually only slips out at races. Even I don't know what he's talking about half the time."

"I get him," Coach Webber said, as he approached the group. He reached out to shake hands with Mom and then waited for Dad, who was just getting himself back up from his squatting position.

Coach and Dad bumped fists, locked thumbs, and wiggled their fingers in the not-so-secret (and in Maryn's opinion, ridiculous) hand-shake they insisted on using to greet each other. Maryn rolled her eyes. Coach was Dad's oldest and best friend. "Loman," Dad said. "You really do superb work coaching these kids. I don't think we tell you often enough."

"Well, they're a great group of athletes," Coach Webber said. "I consider myself lucky." He smiled at Maryn. Pride swelled in her chest for being part of something that Coach considered great.

"Me too," Maryn said. And they *were* lucky he'd decided long ago to devote himself to coaching mountain bike racing right in Redford. *What would we do without him?*

A sharp, clear whistle diverted everyone's attention to the podium.

GOLDEN GIRL

The president of the bike club's board of directors, Pia Bianchi, took the mic. "Welcome, everyone, to the very first race in this season's Ontario Cup cross-country mountain bike racing series," she began over the cheers of the assembled crowd. "It's been our pleasure to host this event right here in Redford. I have to give a big shout-out to our wonderful volunteers—club members and their parents, siblings, aunts, uncles, and even grandparents—who pitched in today to make this event possible. What an excellent start to the season!"

She paused for more cheers, then continued, "The weather has been awesome for early May. We're proud of our trails and, of course, we're proud of our very own racing team, the Radical Off-Roadies."

The audience 'woot wooted' its approval, and then Quentin Dorian, the club's manager, accepted the mic. "I consider myself the head caretaker of these trails," he said. "Today, it is our privilege to share them with athletes from clubs from all over Ontario. I want to remind our local participants and their families that we have a trail repair day next Sunday. Mountain bike racing is always an adventure. And so, without further ado, we will present the medals to today's adventurers."

Maryn's face went back to heating up as she stood on the tallest box to receive her gold medal. Coach Webber's wife, Tomiko Moto (or Tommy, as most people called her), presented Maryn with her medal as everyone—especially her teammates—applauded. Emma Sutcliffe stood beside her to receive the silver. The third place medal went to a girl Maryn recognized from a race last season, but had never actually met. Maryn shook both competitors' hands and then started to step down off the box to leave, but Emma grabbed the rear pocket of her jersey and pulled her back up to give her a heartfelt hug.

"You ruled today, Maryn!" she said.

"Thanks," Maryn said. *Darn! I just got myself out of the spotlight and now here I am on the podium again.* "I think it made a big difference competing on my own trails."

"Maybe...but you were seriously evil out there!" Emma said, and then smiled when Maryn raised her eyebrows. "Meaning excellent," she added.

After the medal presentations, Maryn's teammates and their families headed into the Garage carrying their gear for clean-up and storage. Several of the younger racers crowded around Maryn. Nine-year-old Priya Dhaliwal seemed the most excited. "May I look at your medal?" she asked.

Maryn squatted down to let the little girl take it off.

"May I please try it on?"

"Of course!" Maryn took the medal back from the little girl and then placed it around Priya's neck as if *she* were the gold medallist.

"Are you going to the Olympics?" Priya asked.

"That's the plan. But the Olympics, for me, are still a long way off. I'm only fifteen, and you're not allowed on the Olympic mountain bike racing team until you're nineteen."

"Oh! That does seem like a long way off. Hey, you have really strong legs," she said, pointing at Maryn's muscular thighs. "Mine are so skinny." She studied her own legs and frowned.

"Look over here," Janey took Priya's hand and walked her over to a display case by the main entrance. She pointed to several photos taken over the years of Maryn and her teammates racing and standing on the podium. "See, that's Maryn when she was your age. Look at her legs."

"She had skinny legs just like me!"

"Yup," Maryn said. "Yours will get stronger with lots of hard work. And fun, of course."

"Hey Priya!" called out Joe Brennan, a classmate and long-time member of the Radical Off-Roadies. "Maryn O'Brien is a club legend," he said. "You, Priya Dhaliwal, are hobnobbing with a bona-fide mountain biking legend!"

Oh, no! Not Joe too. Maryn winced.

"I'm not hobnobbing," Priya said, scrunching her nose up at Joe. "What's hobnobbing?" she asked Janey, looking concerned.

"Cut it out, Joe," Maryn scolded.

"I'm serious," he said. "Great race today."

"Thanks. How did it go for you?"

"I got fourth. I had to stop for a few seconds to put my chain back on. It sucked. But it happens."

"Sorry to hear that." Not knowing what else to say, she scanned the tables in the Garage's enormous common area, searching for her family. People kept catching her eye and giving her two thumbs up.

"Killer race today, Maryn," called Charlie Gibson. At eighteen, he was one of the racing team's most senior members.

"You were red-hot out there!" enthused Lydia Bale, who was seventeen and in a different category than Maryn.

Maryn nodded, wanting only to get away from all the attention. Finally, she spotted her parents. Her mom was talking to Gil, and her dad was locking Rocky to the team bike rack at the far end of the Garage.

"Maryn, we have to get going," Mom said, as Maryn joined her and Gil. "I have some work to do at the studio"—Mom owned and operated the Darby O'Brien School of Dance in town—"and your dad has to take Gil to a baseball practice. What are your plans for the day?"

"I'm gonna shower and put away the rest of my gear. Then, after the team briefing, Janey's mom is coming to take us to the barn so we can visit Buddy." Buddy was Janey's twelve-year-old chestnut gelding—a giant horse (by Maryn's estimation) with a calm temperament.

"Okay, honey. We'll see you afterwards," Mom said.

"Great race, Sprint," Dad said.

"Thanks."

"You should be psyched about today," Gil said. "It was quite the season opener."

"Thanks. And thanks for being here."

"It wasn't so bad." He flashed her a small grin.

Her family departed, and then Maryn turned to Janey. "I think I have time for a quick shower before Coach's race debrief."

"Sure." Janey smiled. "I'll just wait here admiring these photos of

Maryn O'Brien, mountain biking legend."

"Argh! Joe Brennan is such a doofus! I'm gonna give him an earful about that. I didn't want to be mean just now when he was telling me about his chain problem."

"Just don't do anything to make Rocky jealous." Janey giggled as Maryn snorted at her and stomped in mock exasperation into the girl's change room.

After stripping down, Maryn hung her towel on a hook on the wall and stepped inside the shower stall, yanking the curtain shut behind her. *I guess people mean well when they make a big deal about my wins,* she thought, turning on the tap. The water spurted out cold, creating instant goose bumps over her entire body. *So why does it bother me so much?* The water stayed cool. She shivered as it cascaded off her curls and down her back. *Maybe it's because I'm scared they're wrong about me. What if I let everybody down?*

COACH'S CORNER

With her sweat and muck showered off, Maryn got Janey settled in the lounge area where she curled up in one of the club's donated sofas with a sci-fi book. The lounge's main purpose was for reviewing race videos. The Garage's decor was simple, its only distinctive feature being the rustic stone chimney of the fireplace built for use during cross-country skiing season. A fridge and large coffee percolator made it possible for the club to run a small canteen during events. The facility, with its change rooms, washrooms, showers, and lockers, allowed the racing team members to store extra gear and shower supplies. Many athletes also kept their bikes locked up there so that they only had to worry about getting themselves to the club for training.

Maryn stepped outside to join the rest of the racing team. About thirty kids sat on a big patch of grass bathed in afternoon sun. Oranges, bananas, and granola bars lay spread out in front of them, leftovers from the post-race snack table. She sat down on the warm grass as Coach Webber began his briefing.

"Well, team, you really showed your stuff today," he said. "The Radical Off-Roadies emerged from a long winter in top form." He paused to let the athletes celebrate with cheers and whistles.

"Now," he said, flipping a page over on his clipboard and getting his pen ready, "since this is the kickoff to a new season, I want to review team expectations. Can I get your help going over the list? Charlie, how 'bout you? Can you start us off by identifying one of our team expectations?"

"Well, we really tear up these paths. So we join in on trail repair days," Charlie said.

"Why yes, we do," Coach said. "Other expectations? Lydia?"

"We make training a priority," she said.

"That's right. But what comes first, ahead of training and racing?"

"Family and school," Lydia said.

"Right. Maryn? What else do we expect of our athletes?" Coach reinforced the racers' responsibilities by reviewing club principles during training and at every race event. He made a point of calling on senior racers to help deliver these messages. Maryn liked how he'd started to call on her, because it showed he'd begun to see her as a leader.

"We come to the scheduled practices ready to work hard," she said. "And we all practice at the same time, in the same way."

"But what if we can't keep up to the big kids?" asked twelve-year-old Melissa Benjamin. She had just joined the team in April. "What if you're all going too far and too fast?"

"Well, Coach adjusts the distances so that you guys can do the same drills and stuff, but finish at the same time as the bikers with more clicks under their belts."

"Clicks?"

"Kilometres," Maryn answered, smiling.

"What else?" Coach probed.

"We set goals and work to achieve them," said Charlie.

"But how?" asked Priya.

"Coach sits down with each of us to help us set good ones," explained Charlie.

"We keep a positive attitude," Joe spoke up. "Like when your chain falls off in the middle of a race." He chucked an orange peel into the brush and let his head drop, sighing. He must have been more upset about the chain incident than he'd let on. But then he raised his head and grinned like the Joe Brennan everyone knew best. "And we cheer each other on."

"I liked it this morning in my race when Maryn screamed my name out by that steep rocky hill," said Priya.

"That's something else I want to remind everybody about," Coach said. "Some of the team's most experienced athletes—Charlie Gibson, Lydia Bale, Maryn O'Brien, and Joe Brennan—will be coaching at our camps this summer. So the newer racers should be geared up about that—if you'll excuse the pun—because it'll give you a break from *me!*" He made a silly face, and then continued, "Before I wrap this up, I want to add one more expectation—the most important one, in my opinion. You come ready to have fun!"

This prompted several whoops from the group, and Coach waited for the noise to die down before going on. "Please keep in mind that our next race in the Ontario Cup series—Georgian Bay—will be in two weeks. Friday will be a driving day, so make sure to let your school teachers know about that. Saturday will be race registration, course familiarization, and bike checks, and Sunday will be race day. Now, let's end this session with a bit of stretching to work out the kinks in all those climbing muscles. We'll start by stretching out our quads."

Maryn closed her eyes and breathed deeply. She savoured the warmth of the sun on her face and the swish of water rushing over rocks in the nearby stream as she contemplated the day's events. Soft grass cushioned her back as she flexed and loosened her sore muscles. The only deeper satisfaction she experienced was when she hid out in her secret sanctuary, but spending time there was rare these days....

BUDDY BUDDY

"Jeesh! Where's my mom?" Janey complained.

The two girls waited in the club parking lot, where Maryn had pulled out the contents of her backpack to reorganize everything. As she did so, a plastic bottle, about the size and shape of a hotel-room shampoo, fell out onto the gravel next to her geography textbook. Its label included a bright yellow lightning bolt emblazoned with the word 'ENERGY.'

"What's that?" Janey asked, picking it up and turning it over to read the front of the bottle. "Energy drops?"

"Oh, yeah, I picked up a multi-pack of those little bottles at the pharmacy a couple of weeks ago," Maryn said. "I think they can give you a boost, like coffee."

"A boost?"

"You know, just enough of a boost to stay on top of things...like my training, my homework, and piano practicing. It can be intense. Plus, all of our final assignments are due this month, and after that, we have exams. Mom and Dad won't let me drink coffee, so I thought I'd give these a try. They were on the shelf along with the sports drinks, so it's no big deal. I dilute them with water like you're supposed to, so it's totally okay."

"Your mom and dad won't let you drink coffee?" Janey asked. "*I've been drinking coffee since I was twelve, not that anybody pays any attention.*"

"They say I'm already 'high strung' and don't need more stimulation. They're also worried it'll keep me from sleeping. You know how much sleep I need, right?"

"Well, yeah. You're totally cranky when you get less than nine hours."

"Am not," said Maryn. Janey acted like such a mother hen sometimes. It was irritating.

"Are so, and you know it!" Janey said. "Whenever you don't get enough sleep, you complain that your workouts suck and you can't concentrate. So, like, maybe your parents have a point?"

"I guess," Maryn said. "But what I *don't* need is a third parent!" She sometimes blurted out 'zingers,' as her mom called them. This happened when she was exhausted, and she was definitely worn out from racing.

The crunch of gravel beneath car tires cut their conversation short, and they both turned to see Janey's mom's Volvo wheel into the parking lot. Maryn stuffed her things back into her bag.

"Sorry I'm late, girls," Mrs. Cunningham said through the open window when they reached the car.

Janey did not say a word in response as she opened the door and plunked herself down onto the front passenger seat.

Maryn caught Mrs. Cunningham's eye in the rear view mirror as she was getting into the back seat, so she felt compelled to say something. "No problem, Mrs. Cunningham, it's a great day to be outside."

"Please. You're old enough to call me Karen now, don't you think?" Janey's mom said. She drove for a few minutes. The silence in the car began to feel awkward until she spoke again. "Maryn, how are things for you at school these days? Have you got a boyfriend?"

"Mom!" Janey exclaimed, "Maryn just competed in an Ontario Cup mountain bike race today. She won a gold medal, and you want to talk about boys? That's messed up."

"Sorry," her mom said, looking back at Maryn and seeming flustered. "Congratulations. That sounds impressive. I was just trying to make a connection, Janey. It's been a long time since I was a fifteen-year-old girl." As she said this, she turned into the long driveway leading to the farm where Janey boarded Buddy.

"Will you be staying?" Janey asked.

"No, I have a ton of work to do before my flight to Chicago. Your Dad will pick you up. Just text him when you're ready."

"Bon voyage," Janey said, in a monotone, as she got out of the car. She didn't look her mom in the eye.

Concerned, Maryn watched her friend closely. She figured Janey was upset with her mom for not staying to watch her ride. "Thanks for driving us Mrs. Cu—I mean, Karen," she said and then jogged to catch up with Janey, who strode towards the barn.

"She could make a connection by staying home for a change," Janey muttered as Mrs. Cunningham drove away. Her eyes welled up with tears, and Maryn wished she hadn't snapped at her earlier. Janey was an only child, so when her mother travelled for work, which was often, it left her either having silent suppers with her father while she 'ninja texted' with Maryn—her term for texting with her phone hidden under the table—or hanging with her cats and sci-fi books while her dad tinkered with the cars in his garage. It also led to Janey eating a lot of suppers at the O'Briens' house. Maryn put her arm around her friend's shoulders as they walked towards the barn.

As they entered the cool, dark stillness of the lofty old structure, Janey took a deep breath. "Ahhh...the sweet smell of manure," she said.

"Whoa, nothing sweet about *that!*" Maryn's voice sounded nasal through her plugged nose.

"You get used to it," Janey said, as she stopped at Buddy's stall and reached into her pack for the bag of carrots she'd been lugging around all morning. "Hi Buddy," she said, looking up at the enormous horse towering over her. She patted the blaze of white on his forehead and fed him carrots with her free hand. "You're my boyfriend, aren't you, Bud?"

"Are we lame?" Maryn asked. When Janey regarded her with raised eyebrows, she asked again, "I mean, well, are we?"

"You mean because we've got Rocky and Buddy instead of actual boyfriends like most of our friends?"

"Well, yeah."

"No. We're doing what's right for *us*." Janey ran a brush down the shiny caramel brown of Buddy's shoulder. "Right now, for me, spending time with Buddy is the best. And the barn is like my second home."

"Hey! I thought *our* place was your second home."

"Nope. Your place *is* home. You don't know how lucky you are to have a family like yours! You have a brother who bothers to come to your races. You have parents who are always there for you. And sometimes you don't even seem happy about it."

Maryn stayed tight-lipped, reflecting on what Janey had said. It was true that she sometimes thought being an only child would rock, and that life would be better if her parents stayed out of her business. But she still felt bad for her friend, and anything she thought of putting into words seemed frivolous. "I'm glad you feel at home with us," she said tentatively. Janey continued silently brushing Buddy, so Maryn talked for a little while, hoping she could cheer her up.

"I was thinking today, when we were in the Garage, about how Dad's bike shop and Mom's dance studio used to be my second homes. I spent so much time hanging out at both places, helping out...taking it all in. But I realized today that the *Garage* is now my second home." Maryn kept chattering until she was sure Janey was feeling better. It was obvious to Maryn, looking at her friend, that just spending time with Buddy was good for Janey.

A few minutes later, Janey had convinced Maryn to ride Buddy bareback. She gave Maryn a boost and helped her get up into a seated position, a tricky manoeuvre without stirrups or saddle, and then jumped up and swung onto Buddy's back behind her, taking up the reins. Buddy easily carried the weight of the two teens, as long as they only wanted to go for a stroll. They rode in silence as Buddy picked his way along the path at the edge of a meadow, the late afternoon sun warm on their shoulders.

"I am so blissed out right now," Maryn eventually said, her body letting go of its tension from the race. "I hardly ever mellow out like this anymore."

"Yeah, you kinda have only one gear these days. Flat out!"

"Yep," Maryn agreed. "I love racing."

"I'm not just talking about when you're racing," Janey said. "You go harder than anyone I know—all the time. In school, music, training, racing..."

"Oh, that's just what my dad calls my O'Brien family work ethic."

"Hm. I don't know about that."

"Hey, speaking of which, I'm starting to freak out about how much work I have to do tonight. I have homework and serious piano practicing to do."

"Why *do* you keep going with your piano lessons, exams, and recitals now that you're so committed to bike racing? Grade nine piano seems to take so much work."

"I know, but I've been playing piano for so long, I honestly don't know how to live without it. It's like I have a battle going on inside me now, between my artistic side and my athletic side. I've worked hard to get where I am in music. Plus, I feel like Mom appreciates not being the lone artist in a house full of sports fanatics," Maryn added.

"Wow. *My* inner battles are over stuff like pizza or Chinese food—which will I order tonight?" Janey made a show of pretending to look thoughtful, and both girls laughed. Then she continued, "Okay, okay. I'll text my dad and we'll get you home for your Sunday night cram-fest."

"Thanks." Maryn patted Buddy on his powerful neck. As the horse ambled back to the barn, she considered Janey's words and questions. She hadn't been entirely honest with her friend, because there was so much more to her inner battles than just artist versus athlete. But she didn't dare talk about it to Janey—or to anyone—because if people knew how messed up she was inside, they wouldn't think she was fit to be an Olympian.

But she was. And all she had to do was prove it to Coach.

FIVE TO GO

Two weeks later, Maryn posted her second win of the season at the Georgian Bay race.

She and her dad had carpooled to the race with Coach Webber and two other team members. Maryn's mom had stayed home to cover weekend dance classes and drive Gil to his baseball games, and the Off-Roadies had left late Friday morning and driven for most of the day. They'd spent Saturday registering, familiarizing themselves with the course, and adjusting their bikes for the terrain, for the race on Sunday.

By the time Coach Webber had returned them home at eight on Sunday evening, it had been a very long day. Maryn had been up since six in the morning, warmed up, won the gruelling twelve-kilometre race, cheered on her teammates, stayed for the medal presentations, and helped load up the bikes and gear. Then she'd ridden in a van for five and a half hours with only one quick stop for gas, a bathroom break, and take-out food. Now she lay on her bed—limp and incapable of moving.

She had tried to nap in the van, but had not succeeded, feeling almost hyper-energized. She had, however, managed to listen to several chapters of a book she had downloaded onto her smartphone. She needed to read it for an English essay that was due soon, and Gil had suggested she buy the audio book.

"It's not cheating, Maryn," he'd urged. *"You need to multi-task because of everything you're into right now. It's a good way to use your travel time."*

Maryn sometimes hated that Gil was so smart. "Wise beyond his years," her dad always said.

Maryn fumed as she lay on her bed. Everything seemed to come so easily to Gil. Not just school, but sports too. *He's even prettier than me,* she thought. *He looks just like Mom with that cool combo of spiky black hair and blue eyes.* She, on the other hand, had inherited her dad's unruly sandy-brown hair and hazel (not green, blue, or brown) eyes.

At the time Gil had suggested she listen to audio books, she had jumped down his throat, growling, *"I'm not gonna listen to somebody reading me a book like I'm some little kid being read a bedtime story!"* But within an hour, after she reviewed her homework situation, she had reconsidered and downloaded the book—a three hundred and fifty-plus pager—read by Benedict Cumberbatch. She wished she could have told Gil it was a good idea. But her pride had gotten the better of her...she didn't want him thinking he was smarter than his big sister.

She lay lifeless on her bed for about ten minutes before managing to coax herself upright. Her room wasn't big, but it was her own space, and she'd put her personal stamp on it. She'd chosen a deep green paint for the walls and ceiling, and lots of natural wood—a pine floor and handmade pine bed, side table, dresser, and bookshelves. The race posters she'd put up all around her made it feel as if she was still biking in the woods.

Her race countdown calendar covered the wall at the foot of her bed. She'd placed it there for immediate viewing in the mornings before she got up and in the evenings right before she went to sleep. That way, her race schedule would be imprinted on her brain, something she believed helped focus her energy.

She scanned the seven Ontario Cup Series races listed on the calendar—two in May, two in June, and one in each of July, August, and September. Her eyes zeroed in on the September race, the Provincial Championships. She jumped up, grabbed a marker from her dresser, and put a big check mark beside the Georgian Bay race. "Two down...five to go," she murmured. A surge of panic took hold of her. Summer vacation began in just six weeks, and she still had two more races, a piano exam, a ton of school work, and finals. How would she ever manage? She took a deep, calming breath, then plucked a thumb tack from her bookshelf and pinned up the ribbon holding her Georgian Bay gold medal right next to her Redford gold medal. She sat back on her bed and regarded them. Displaying the two golds in her private space helped keep her centred, reminding her she was already two steps closer to her Olympic goal. But her sense of victory was short-lived.

She'd beaten Emma that morning, but barely. And now she was dead tired, but still had to practice piano tonight. She'd been away from her piano since early Friday morning when she'd gotten about an hour and a half of practicing done before leaving for Georgian Bay, and she still had a lot of memory work to do before her next lesson.

She reached into her bag to find her energy drops. *This is the only way I'm gonna be able to keep my eyes open tonight*, she told herself, dribbling almost double the recommended number of drops into her water bottle before carrying it with her to the piano room down on the main floor. The ten-foot square space had a single tiny window and contained an upright piano and bench, a hard plastic straight-back chair, a loveseat, and a bookshelf filled with music. It wasn't fancy, but it served its purpose. Closing the door behind her, Maryn took a sip of the enhanced water. As she swallowed, she wondered if the drops might have kept her from sleeping in the van, but she pushed the idea away. *Ah well*, she thought. *Sometimes you've gotta do what you've gotta do.*

SCHOOL SCOOP

The next morning, Monday, Maryn shuffled into the kitchen at seven thirty.

"Maryn, you look bone weary." Dad tousled her massive mess of hair.

"Mm-hm," Maryn mumbled, in a fog. She had made her way over to the coffee maker where a full pot had been freshly brewed. She reached up into the cupboard above the machine, grabbed a mug, and started pouring.

"Whoa now, Missy!" Dad warned, looking up from spreading peanut butter on his toast. "Whaddya think you're doing?"

"I guess I'm pouring *you* a cup of coffee." She pouted.

"Maryn, I know you're tired, but your mom and I have discussed this with you, and we all agreed that since you get so wired—even without the stimulus of caffeine—and because of your very real need for sleep to support your training and racing, coffee consumption's just a bad idea, right?"

"Uh-huh."

"And Coach has also cautioned you against it because it's a diuretic. Remember? It helps rid your body of fluids. You know as an athlete you need to stay hydrated, so getting rid of fluids is the opposite of what you want, right?"

"I know, I get it." As she poured herself a bowl of granola, Gil breezed into the kitchen, freshly showered and dressed for school. Smiling, he reached in front of Maryn to grab an apple from the old stoneware mixing bowl on the counter that they kept filled with fruit.

"Don't *you* look all shiny and happy?" Maryn goaded her brother. "Always ready to start your perfect day with a smile." Her sarcasm hung in the air like the mist from a sneeze. *Uh oh, more zingers*, she thought. She was worn-out, late, and worried about school, and as usual, Gil had everything under control.

Gil bit hard into his apple and sized her up as he chewed. "The flannel boxers are a good look for you," he observed around his mouthful. "Is that drool on your giant tee? Nice touch. I hear that's a thing now, tee-shirt drool stains."

Maryn glared at her brother, but she had lost her will to carry on the mean exchange she'd started.

"Maryn, have a good, I mean, messed-up day. Dad, see ya later." Gil left the house, whistling.

"What was that all about?" Her mom entered the kitchen as the door closed behind Gil. "It sounded like an unhappy start to the day. Do you think it could have gone differently?"

"I guess. If you had different kids," Maryn muttered.

"We know you're tired, but you still have to try to be civil. We're a family. We care for each other."

"It must suck for you to have one nice kid, and then me!"

"*I* kinda like ya." Her dad beamed for a moment, and then resumed reading his newspaper.

Maryn sat smouldering on a tall wooden stool at their island breakfast bar. Her parents had designed the eat-in kitchen to be like Dad's grandparents' country kitchen. He had great memories of lively family meals there, so he and Mom wanted their own kitchen to be the heart of their home too. They'd used old boards salvaged from the O'Brien farm to make a rustic countertop for the island, and Maryn loved the mismatched cabinet knobs from the old farmhouse kitchen. The wide planked floor, hanging copper pots, and deep sink where the morning sunlight streamed in almost always brightened her mood.

Today, however, she could not be cheered. She'd been awful to Gil. She'd disappointed her mom. Her piano-practicing the night before had seemed desperate and futile. And she couldn't remember what was happening at school today. She thought about texting Janey to find out, but decided to get going instead. *I'll get the rundown from her before first period,* she thought. There had to be at least one benefit to having an annoyingly organized brainiac for a best friend.

***

"Janey!" Maryn called out as she arrived at her locker, relieved to see that her friend was still at hers, just two over.

"Hey Maryn." Janey eyed her with concern. "You look beat. Rough night?"

"Sketchy sleep, I guess. Do we have French first period?"

"Oh yeah. Madame Adams. And I'm pretty sure she'll be treating us to a 'random' dictée."

"Are you kidding me?"

"Wassup?" asked Omar Habib, who had just arrived at his locker across the hall from them. "Did you say we have a French vocabulary test?"

"Yep," Janey said. "I'm on to her. I've been mapping out her method and her dictées are *way* less random than she'd like us to believe."

"What's the pattern?" Omar asked, seeming interested in Janey's mapping of Madame Adams' testing quirks. Maryn herself was much less fascinated.

I'm so gonna suck at a vocabulary test today, she thought. The prospect of a poor result put her in an even worse mood. As she, Janey and Omar entered Madame Adams' classroom, Maryn noticed Joe Brennan across the room, sitting on Tracey Jennings' desk.

"He sure works hard at getting Tracey to like him," Maryn grumbled to Janey as they took their seats.

"Aw, he's a nice guy. And I think Tracey does like him. He's pretty cute with all those muscles and his shaggy blond surfer hair. He must be fun to have on your racing team."

Tracey laughed at Joe's antics while trying to hide her braces with a French paperback. Maryn frowned.

"Joe bugs me sometimes."

"Why?"

"I think he's lazy."

"Really?"

"Yeah. He misses practices. And when he does come, he always seems way more concerned about being an entertaining doofus than about doing any real work. I get kinda miffed when he ends up on the podium."

"That's pretty harsh. You *must* be tired!"

Maryn sighed and then turned sideways to face Janey at the desk beside her. "Okay, okay, you're right," she said, now whispering as more students filed into the classroom. "I think it's because Joe reminds me of Gil and how easy things seem to come to him. I feel like I work so hard all the time, and they just cruise through everything, but they still always seem to pull off the big win."

"Why do you care so much?" Janey whispered back. "I mean, they aren't your real competition, are they?"

"I guess it's because I started biking with Dad so young that when I joined the racing team, there weren't many girls with my kind of experience. So, most days, I ended up training with the guys. Race results are posted by category, but I train with Joe and live with Gil. In my mind, they *are* the competition."

Joe hopped down from Tracey's desk when Madame Adams entered the room. As the teacher began unpacking her bag, Joe nodded at Maryn from two rows over. "Congratulations on grabbing another gold in Georgian Bay, Maryn," he said. "You were scorchin' fast."

Before Maryn could respond, Julie Davis and Stephanie Harwood stopped in front of Joe's desk and eyed Maryn, managing to appear both inquisitive and bored at the same time.

"A gold medal, Maryn?" Stephanie questioned. "How sweet. Was that in one of your little dirt bike races?" She smirked.

"*Mountain* bike," Maryn corrected.

"As editor, I might assign Julie the task of writing a feature article on that for the *J.T. Seeley Collegiate Online Review,*" Stephanie said, "or not." She rolled her eyes and continued toward her desk.

"It's actually a pretty big deal, Steph," Joe said. "Maryn's hard core."

"Maybe she's just a big fish in your tiny bike club pond," Julie said.

"Maybe she should consider devoting more time to reining in that mane." Stephanie pointed at Maryn's hair. A few students snickered.

Maryn had forgotten she'd let her wild hair free in her rush to see Janey before class. She refrained from smoothing it down. She and Janey had both stopped liking those two girls in grade three when they'd started up a princess club that rejected certain people. She refused to let them get to her now.

She glanced away from them and caught Liam Gallagher's eye. Liam, like Janey, had been in her class since junior kindergarten. "I like the mane," he said with a grin.

Maryn grabbed the hair tie she'd placed on her wrist as she'd run out of the house that morning and twisted her curls back into a thick loopy ponytail.

"It sounds like your training's paying off," Liam said.

Maryn smiled and shrugged. Uncomfortable with more attention on her racing wins, she changed the subject. "How's the rowing? I noticed you finishing up some training on the track this morning when I got here."

"Yeah, that's right. I was doing some speed work. Things are shaping up pretty well this season."

"Do you race solo or do you have a partner? I can't remember."

"I'm a single sculler."

"Any big races coming up?"

"Yeah, a regatta in Welland in a couple of weeks."

"Well, good luck."

"Thanks. Same."

That's weird, she thought. *I don't think I've really talked to Liam Gallagher since, um, grade five.*

Janey was right about the vocabulary test. Afterwards, Madame Adams asked the students to mark each others' work. Julie checked Maryn's.

"Fifty percent." She held the paper up for Stephanie to see and pointed at Maryn.

"Maybe the real story in the *Review* should be about jocks and smarts...how the two rarely intersect," Stephanie taunted.

Maryn made a face and turned towards Janey. "The only way she learns anything about jocks is by dating them." She was bummed about her lousy mark, but even more bummed about Julie and Stephanie trying to shame her.

"I know, right?" Janey snickered. "Aren't they both going to the spring formal with grade twelve guys from the basketball team?"

"Yeah," Maryn said. "Stephanie and Julie, the first-ever grade nine 'co-representatives' on student council and the first grade nines in charge of organizing the formal. Plus, Stephanie is the first-ever grade nine editor of the *Review*. How does that stuff happen? They aren't even nice to teachers!"

"I guess they *make* it happen."

"Hmph. I just hope they keep using their powers for the good, kinda, because those two are hungry and get nasty when they turn on you."

RAVE REVIEW

Maryn's stomach churned—like she had hunger pains that wouldn't go away. It was a Sunday afternoon at the beginning of June. Her third Ontario Cup race of the season was in exactly one week, and her grade nine piano exam was two days after that.

She and Coach Webber sat on the Garage sofa watching video footage from the Georgian Bay race. "I had Tommy record everyone on that bony climb coming up from the creek, remember?" he asked.

Maryn nodded. She'd spent enough time with both her dad and Coach Webber to know that 'bony' meant rocky in old guy mountain-biking lingo. And now that he mentioned it, she did recall Coach's wife, Tommy, filming from the top of the rise.

"Okay, watch how you tackle it. Look. Perfect technique." He froze the picture on a frame showing the power in Maryn's legs and the efficient form she used to get up the steepest section of the twisty hill. "You control your speed beautifully, using momentum from the previous downhill, standing up at just the right time, and then taking that very tight turn at the top with care and control. Excellent job!"

"Rocky should get some credit," Maryn suggested. "He's designed to deal with those conditions."

"Sure, but if the biker in charge doesn't have the technique to handle it, then a bike's design won't help. Now look—here comes Emma." He pointed at the laptop and played more of the video. "As you can see, she did *not* have the same mastery of this hill. That might've been where she lost the race right there."

Maryn squinted at the screen. To see herself do things right gave her a concrete image to focus on when she tackled hills in her next races. She began nodding her understanding, but just then, metal hit concrete with a resounding crash. Maryn flinched as though somebody had sneaked up behind her and smashed a set of cymbals, but it was only someone dropping a bicycle pump over by the bike stands.

"Jumpy?" Coach Webber asked. "You seem a bit more on edge than usual. Are you sleeping okay?"

"Um, well, no, not great," she said. "I've been staying up late to practice piano. Coach, do you think you'll give me the go-ahead to do some Canada Cup races next season? I mean, do you think two golds is a sign that I'm ready?"

"I know you're anxious to get onto that circuit, Maryn. But this season isn't just about winning golds. It's about showing me what you can handle. It's all about making sure you're ready—in body *and* mind—to handle the load. Canada Cup racing will involve more travel and the competition will be fierce. Let's see how it goes, okay?"

Maryn's heart sank into her agitated stomach. Coach was in her corner. But getting the go-ahead from him today would have taken a huge load off her mind. She was wigging out about the month of June with her next two races...the first, right before her piano exam, and the second before her high school exams. She waited for a moment or two, inhaled deeply and then took a risk. "Coach, what do you think about me using those energy drops you see all over the place now?"

"Hey! You know there's no substitute for a good night's sleep and excellent nutrition. I'm very much against the use of artificial stimulants."

Maryn's face burned. What would Coach do if he found out that she'd been using them for weeks?

"I'm okay with athletes taking in the odd energy drink when depleted from an endurance race or a long hot training session," he continued. "You know, to replace lost electrolytes. But other than that, no way. Remember, you need to find a balance in your life. You do that by prioritizing, perhaps dropping something that may be causing you to feel overloaded. Not by taking drops to give you a manufactured boost. Making good decisions will be a part of showing me you're ready to advance to the next level."

***

Maryn sat alone and on the verge of tears in the O'Brien's piano room. She was going over a tough section of her Brahms prelude, and she could not work out the problems in the challenging passage. It seemed the more time she spent on it, the worse she got.

"Argh! Why do I even try anymore?" she wailed out loud. "I have the energy of a sloth and the brainpower of a mosquito."

Coach Webber's words rang in her ears. She had always done exactly what he told her to do; she believed it was the recipe for success. He had guided her towards achieving every single mountain-biking goal she had ever set for herself. But she was faltering at the piano, and could hardly keep her eyes open. She was about to ignore her coach's very clear statement that he was against her taking the energy drops.

She had a tall glass of water at the piano and a bottle of drops in the pocket of her hoodie. Coach was probably right about the drops, but then again, this was just temporary, right? What Dad called a quick fix—something to get her through this month from hell.

She took the little bottle out of her pocket and held it over the glass of water, at first counting the clear drops as they came out. But then she squeezed hard and let a stream of the liquid cascade into the glass. She had used more than four times the recommended dose and was now about to drink the equivalent of six cups of coffee. She put the glass to her lips and downed the entire mixture at once. She held her hands out in front of her. They shook. Was it the thought of brushing off her coach? Or was it the drops?

Maryn returned to the problem passage. "At least I'll be able to stay awake long enough to nail this section once and for all," she said to the empty room. *But at what cost?* responded a voice in her head.

PANIC ATTACK

The next Ontario Cup race was in Barrie, another five-hour drive from Redford. Gil had come along this time, in part because he and Dad had gotten tickets for a Toronto Blue Jays game that night. Mom had remained at home to run dance performance rehearsals.

Maryn had opted not to go to the ball game. She'd stayed back at the hotel, which was just north of Toronto, to get some studying done and turn in early. It was Friday night. She stabbed her last forkful of ravioli. Dad had suggested she order a pasta dish and a salad from room service. She texted Janey.

"you home?"

"ha! where else? where r u?"

"hotel nowhere"

"crashing soon?"

"still studying, you?"

"done"

"everything?"

"yep. I'm ready"

"I wish"

"want help?"

"wanna write my exams for me?"

"LOL"

"k gotta go"

"good luck"

"thanks"

Maryn sighed and turned off her phone. She was far from ready for exams next week. In a way, she wished she hadn't texted her friend. *Compared to Janey I'm a bonehead*, she thought. But it was definitely good to talk to someone who cared about her. Unable to fall asleep, and feeling a bit sorry for herself, she regretted not going to the game with the guys.

***

On Saturday morning, they drove another hour to the race site, which was at a ski resort just outside of Barrie. Maryn did a short practice ride on the race course while they waited for Coach Webber and the other Radical Off-Roadies to arrive. Dad and Gil came along since they'd brought three bikes. Riding with the O'Brien 'boys' reminded Maryn of how much fun she and Gil had always had as young kids pedalling after their dad all over the trails in Redford. And activating her childhood joy for the sport gave her a genuine boost.

Once registration ended, Coach took all of the Off-Roadies out on the course to analyze it and discuss strategy. Afterwards, Maryn visualized every bump and bend of the once unfamiliar trails; on the night before her race, that was exactly what she needed to do.

***

Sunday. Race day. Maryn woke with adrenaline already surging through her veins. She was ready for this. She had to be ready for it.

She was dressed and organized well before Gil and her dad, chomping at the bit to get going. Breakfast consisted of a bagel with cream cheese and a nectarine, which she choked down past the knot in her throat, knowing she needed the nutrients for the race even if she didn't feel like eating. At last they were on their way.

When they arrived at the site, Maryn warmed up with the team. Just before her age group assembled for the start, Coach Webber jogged up to her and tapped on the front of her helmet. "How're you feeling?" he asked, assessing her overall state. He gave her a quick shoulder massage.

"I'm solid," she said, and then stood on her right upper pedal and swung her left leg up over her seat to glide over to join the other bikers.

At the starting line, she took a moment to locate her primary competitors, Emma Sutcliffe and the girl who had nabbed third place at the Redford race in May. She couldn't remember the girl's name, but man, she had legs on her. She had to be at least six feet tall. Maryn turned her attention back to the ground in front of her, muscles tensed, waiting for the starting pistol.

Crack! The sound ricocheted over their heads, and almost as one, the group of bikers surged forward.

Maryn positioned herself off to one side and towards the front of the throng, but she fell back a bit off the start when her wheels slipped in deep gravel. She pushed hard to get herself up with Emma and the new girl, then tucked in directly behind them just as the open expanse of the parking lot narrowed to a wooded single track.

They entered the forest. All three of them grunted like weight lifters bracing for their next powerlift. They rode hard, Emma in front, New Girl right behind Emma, and Maryn behind New Girl. She could blow past both of them in the clearing just beyond the next climb. All she had to do was breathe down New Girl's neck and wait for it.

But suddenly, Maryn's focus shifted. Her heart pounded out of control, and a wave of nausea passed through her—something that only ever happened when she had over-trained or been on the verge of heat stroke. Alarmed to feel like this just eight minutes into the race, she allowed herself to fall back a couple of metres. She gave her head a shake, took a few deep breaths, then hammered hard on her pedals to close the gap. The forest floor rose up sharply on an incline. The change in grade threw her off, and she changed gears out of sync with her gravity-stalled pace. The chain slipped and jammed. She needed to get off the bike to recover, but instead she tried a desperate move to pop the chain loose anyway. She failed. Her chain snapped, and she turned sharply to get her bike off the course as several other riders flew up the rise.

Maryn inspected the damage. She had only broken a chain once before. She owned a tool for repairing it, but hadn't carried it with her for a race of eleven-and-a-half kilometres. If it had been a fifty-kilometre event, it might have been worth it to fix the chain and continue racing for the top spot, but in a race of this distance, Maryn's mistake had cost her dearly. All she could do now was wait for the rest of the competitors to pass and then push her bike in the opposite direction all the way back to the starting area. She jogged for most of it and got herself back in about fifteen minutes.

She waved her father down as she ran her bike over to the officials' table. Her dad had read her mind and was already on his way over with a replacement bike.

The lead riders had just come out of the bush and raced past the spectators. The officials gave Maryn the go-ahead to join back in as they began their second loop. She tucked in behind the largest pack.

When the lead riders charged for the finish, Maryn still had to complete her second loop. Melissa and Priya cheered as she headed off to begin it solo.

"Go Maryn!" they shrieked. Afterwards, it was the little girls who greeted her at the finish.

"Maryn, what happened?" asked Priya. "Did your bike break?"

"Yep, my chain broke." Maryn took off her helmet.

"I think it's so cool that you finished the race anyway," said Melissa.

"Yeah," agreed Priya. "*Very* cool."

Maryn smiled at her younger teammates. "That's what Radical Off-Roadies do, right? We come to race," she said, as Gil, her dad, and Coach Webber approached. She turned to her coach. "I made a ridiculous mistake, Coach."

Before anyone could respond, Emma called over from where she was cleaning off her bike. "Sorry about your bad luck, Maryn!"

"Thanks Emma," Maryn said, appreciating that her rival had given her the benefit of the doubt and called it bad luck. "Good job on *your* race," she added, forcing a smile.

"Keeping your composure under these circumstances and being a great role model for your young teammates showed enormous maturity, Maryn," Coach Webber said. "We'll do some race analysis later. For now, let's get over to cheer the other Off-Roadies."

Gil took Maryn's bike, and Dad put his arm around her as they walked towards the starting area. Maryn felt a bit better after hearing Coach's positive words, but the truth was, she'd panicked out there and behaved like an inexperienced biker. What was happening to her?

WTH?

Maryn lay in bed, scanning the race calendar across the room. It was Wednesday morning, the day after her piano exam, and Hardwood Hills, the last race before the end of grade nine, was just around the corner. She was glad to have the piano exam behind her, but her stomach convulsed when she thought about her final exams for school.

A ding sounded. She glanced over to where her smartphone sat charging on her bedside table. It was a text from Janey. She picked it up to read it.

"how'd the exam go?"

"pretty good," Maryn typed.

"yay!"

"I choked at one point, tho, can I call u?"

"yup"

Maryn picked up her phone and touched Janey's name in her favourites list. Janey picked up in half a ring.

"Hey," Maryn said.

"Hey! I was worried about you. I called, like, a bazillion times."

"I turned off my phone and conked early after the exam. I barely even talked to my family. I think I was comatose by seven."

Maryn found Janey's mother hen routine irritating, but then she remembered that Janey had plenty of experience watching her get all keyed up about exams, festivals, and recitals. She was just trying to be a good friend.

"You said you choked?"

"Yeah, in the opening of the prelude, I just froze. But the guy was so nice about it. He let me walk outside in the garden to calm down and then restart."

"How'd it go after that?"

"Really great. I mean, I got through it with decent technique and no more memory gaps after I got over the freezing thing. So I'm revved up. And I'm even more revved up to have it done! Janey, I know I'm a bear in the lead-up to these things. You sure put up with a lot when I drag you onto my emotional roller coaster—'Yay, I signed up to do another exam. Waahhh, I'm panicking.'"

"That's okay. It's always an interesting ride."

"See you at school?"

"See ya."

***

As Maryn approached her desk in French class, Stephanie and Julie stepped towards her.

"Guess what, jock?" Stephanie asked Maryn, wearing an odd smile.

Maryn refused to respond.

"I think you're gonna love this!" Julie piped up, her tone sopping with sarcasm.

"We're both gonna join your strange little world this summer," Stephanie said. "We're joining your so-called Radical Off-Whatevers."

"Roadies," Julie said.

"Whatever."

Maryn had paused at her desk. She could not take in what Stephanie and Julie were saying to her.

"We're joining your bike club right after finals," Julie said. "We've signed up as members for July and August, and if we like it, we'll extend our memberships into the fall."

Maryn stood frozen, taken aback. Maybe they were joking. They *had* to be joking.

"We're looking for new experiences," Stephanie explained with a fake smile. "We're getting tired of dating basketball stars, you know? And Charlie Gibson *is* kinda cute."

Maryn gawped at Joe, trying to make some sense of this, but Joe just shrugged and grinned his Joe Brennan grin. Would Stephanie and Julie end up being in one of her summer camp sessions? Would they be taking her Learn to Ride clinic? Could they even ride mountain bikes? What was this about?

***

At lunch, Maryn was about to begin ranting on the topic of Julie and Stephanie's announcement, when Janey spoke first. "Did you hear about those kids over at Maple Grove High School?" she asked.

"What kids?"

"The kids who ended up in the hospital because of taking those energy drops."

"What?"

"They were daring each other to pound them back. You know, slamming them back like they were chugging twenty coffees all at once. There were about five of them doing it. Two girls ended up in emergency."

"With what?"

"I don't know. Like, weird heart rhythms, I think. And, um, one of them had a seizure. They were really sick anyway. Are you still taking them?"

"Sometimes," Maryn said. "But I'm not being stupid about it. I'm diluting them like you're supposed to."

"I think you should stop taking them."

"Well, I think I should *keep* taking them. I know what I'm doing!"

"What did Coach Webber say about it?"

"He's fine with it," Maryn lied.

"Well, what did he say *exactly*?"

"He said it's *fine*, so let's drop it!" Maryn's heart raced, maybe because she was angry with Janey for butting in, maybe because she'd lied to her best friend, or maybe because she was taking the drops. Whatever the reason, she feared her racing heart would never slow down again.

On Friday, Principal Topping announced that energy drops like the ones taken by the students at Maple Grove High School were no longer permitted on school property. "After today, any J.T. Seeley Collegiate student found to have these drops on school premises will be suspended," she stated. "This is a zero tolerance policy, so be smart about it."

Janey looked pointedly at the water bottle on Maryn's desk, then at Maryn. Maryn's face warmed a bit as she stared back at her friend. Technically, the policy didn't come into effect until Monday.

SUMMER BREEZE

Hardwood Hills, Maryn's last race of the school year, went much better than Barrie had, but Emma still edged her out to claim first place, making it two golds for each of them in the series. Maryn had kept the lead for the first of three loops, but when Emma surged ahead in the middle of the second loop, she couldn't dig deep enough to answer back. Her heart rate climbed so high that she panicked and lost her composure. In the time it took to calm down, Emma had gained a solid enough lead to hold on until the finish. New Girl had not been racing, so the third place finisher had been a significant distance back. Once again, Maryn wondered if the energy drops were causing the spike in her heart rate, and once again, she told herself they were just what she needed to train harder and better.

Exams came and went. Maryn had managed not to take her energy drops at school since Principal Topping's announcement, but she continued taking them at night to get her through her finals. Despite her extracurricular schedule and worry, she made honour roll for grade nine.

When school and piano ended for the summer, mountain bike training intensified. As Coach had promised, the club recruited Maryn to lead Learn to Ride clinics and work at their summer day camps. She usually coached small groups of young girls who were new to mountain biking. She was glad to be at the club so often and managed to do some level of her own training almost every day.

"Are you sure you should be taking on these camps and clinics?" her mom asked, checking in with her a couple of weeks into the summer. "They must be physically draining. Wouldn't you rather help Dad out at the bike shop or play piano for some of my summer dance classes to earn a bit of money?"

"No, Mom. It's less about the money and more about staying in touch with my bike and my trails. The camps and the clinics are exactly what I want to be doing. Honest." She spoke the truth to her mother, and she even stopped using the energy drops for a time. With only one race on the calendar in mid-July and one in August, she was closer to finding the balance Coach Webber had talked about back in the spring. She was certain of it.

Summer also gave Maryn the chance to retreat more often to her secret sanctuary—a place that provided peace, privacy, and comfort, but above all, connected her with nature. She'd discovered it at age twelve while kicking a soccer ball along a hiking trail near her house. Frustrated about losing a 'friendly' game of one-on-one with Gil, she'd kicked the ball hard and caused it to disappear into the brush between the trail and the river. She'd picked her way through a thicket and found her ball resting in the dappled shade of a sugar maple grove. The trees stood straight and tall, and when she looked up, she felt as if she were in a church. She later discovered that she could sit unseen beneath the branches. The dense shrubs growing between the maple forest and the path created a buffer between Maryn and the world (or, at least, between Maryn and those who walked the path), and the place became her safe haven. She could go there to think, dream, shed tears, or even just soak up the sounds and smells of the wild space.

One warm evening shortly after Maryn's July race, Janey came along with the family to watch one of Gil's baseball games. Maryn and Janey sat high in the stands, chatting.

"I actually find Gil's games relaxing," Maryn said. She stretched out her legs and leaned back to get comfortable on the hard metal seat, then pointed to a group of girls in the stands below, who screamed and cheered for Gil while he pitched. "Watch that bunch."

"There's Zoe Jovanovic," said Janey. She pointed out Gil's girlfriend.

Maryn had teased him about Zoe, but he hadn't opened up to say they were officially going together. "Yeah," she said. "She's been to quite a few games this summer. She's not just a groupie like some of those other flakes. She's an amazing soccer player. And Gil goes to lots of her games too."

Janey glanced sideways at her. "You seem much less, um, intense these days."

"I know. I feel better when I don't have racing and school and piano. The Albion Hills race felt good and I'm finally well rested."

"Where's Albion Hills, again?"

"It's not far from Toronto. They have the race in a conservation area there."

"You won that one, right?"

"I did. But Emma wasn't there, which I didn't expect, since she lives so close by in Newmarket. I'd feel a bit better if I'd also beaten *her*. Do you remember the new girl that came in third here in Redford?"

Janey nodded.

"Well she was really close behind me at Albion Hills for a while. I held her off, but it wasn't easy. I talked to her after the race. She moved to Ontario from Alberta in the middle of last season. Her name's Brooklyn Morrison. Anyway, at least I rode smart and kept everything together. The August race will matter, but I'm pretty sure the deciding factor for Coach will be the big one in September."

"Is that the Provincial Championships?"

"Exactly."

"How far do you have to travel for that?"

"We hardly have to travel at all. It's at the little ski resort just outside of Redford. I'd say a forty-minute drive at most. If I win that race, I'm sure Coach will let me compete in the Canada Cup series. It will be a whole new level of racing, but I know I can do it. It's the next step for me, and I'm ready."

"Ew." Janey scrunched up her nose. "With the big race happening so close to Redford, I'll have to go."

"You don't *have* to do anything!" Maryn gave Janey an affectionate shove, and her friend shrugged in return.

"I want to be a supportive friend," she responded.

"That's nice. But I don't want you to have a nervous breakdown."

"It's okay. Nervous breakdowns build character."

***

A few nights later, when Janey came over for supper, Maryn cautiously asked how things were going between her and her mom.

"It's hard to tell, really." Janey followed her around the table, putting forks beside the plates Maryn set down. "You actually have to spend time together to know how things are."

"So she's still travelling a lot? Even in the summer? Won't you guys take a family vacation or something?"

"Maryn, we're not the O'Briens!" Janey snapped. "Let's see, when was the last time we took a family vacation? Was it New York in April? Nope. Mom cancelled that trip because of an emergency meeting in Oslo. Was it the cottage rental this summer in the Kawarthas? Nope, Mom cancelled because work couldn't live without her."

"That sucks," Maryn said, feeling a sudden surge of gratitude for her own family.

"It's okay." Janey shrugged one shoulder as she folded napkins. "Summers for me mean spending lots of time with Buddy. At least *he's* reliable."

Maryn might have pursued the conversation further, but just then her dad sailed into the room with a platter of burgers and a booming, "So who's hungry?"

The ordinary chaos of supper ensued. Janey sat next to Maryn, as she usually did, with Zoe next to Gil, and Mom and Dad at opposite ends of the oversized harvest table.

"This has become a bad habit," Maryn whispered to Janey.

"What has?"

"Zoe being over here for supper."

"She seems to fit in great!"

"Yeah." Maryn watched Zoe and her brother tussling over a jar of mustard. "You're right about that."

"So how are you coping with being around Stephanie and Julie so much since they've joined the bike club?" Janey asked, now talking above the clatter at the table.

"It's painful." Maryn made a face.

"Stephanie Harwood and Julie Davis?" asked Zoe.

"Oh yeah." Gil snorted. "Believe me, we've been hearing about it!"

"Seriously, though, Gil, why did Stephanie and Julie join a mountain bike racing team?" Maryn challenged. "I mean, come *on*!"

"Hey, aren't you club ambassador or something? Isn't it your job to share the joys of mountain biking with new riders of all ages?"

Maryn glowered. "All they do is complain about the workouts. 'Hill repeats? We don't *do* hill repeats,'" she mimicked. "And 'This is soooo boring.' They're slower than...than...well, let's just say that they're not in great shape. Coach had me working with them on the long climb up to the hydro line and they were going so slowly I could hardly keep my bike upright. They're hopeless."

"What are hill repeats, exactly?" Janey cut short Maryn's rant.

"They're just what you'd think, really...climbing the same hill over and over again to learn techniques for tackling hills. But also to build endurance for hilly race courses."

"I hope they don't know you feel that way," Dad said, looking at her with concern. "Gil's right, you know, it *is* one of your jobs to help the developmental riders. And even though Stephanie and Julie have come to the sport late, they still deserve any help you can give."

"Um, Mr. O'Brien?" Janey chimed in. "I'm pretty sure those girls joined the bike club mainly to irk Maryn."

"Seriously?" asked Mom.

"Well, there's probably more to it than that. But for sure it's an added bonus for them to invade Maryn's world."

"Hmm...'mean girl' stuff?" Dad asked.

"Well, yeah. I think those two resent the fact that Maryn is the queen of something. That's usually their thing."

"I can see that," Zoe said.

"Yeah. Maybe they're hoping to dethrone Queen Stress Case," said Gil.

Despite the annoyance factor of Stephanie and Julie, Maryn felt so light-hearted these days that she didn't even challenge Gil on his stress case remark.

* * *

Later that evening, with her newest gold medal in hand, Maryn once again sat on the end of her bed contemplating her race calendar. The recent Albion Hills race had been the fifth of seven races. She hadn't won a medal in Barrie, where she had broken her chain, but she'd won two gold medals (Redford and Georgian Bay) and one silver (Hardwood Hills) in the series so far. Fierce determination flooded over her as she added the Albion Hills gold to the July date with a tack. *Not bad,* she thought, looking at her four medals. *I'm getting there.*

ACTIVE RECOVERY

"Too hard, Maryn!" boomed Joe's voice from behind her. He'd ridden up with Coach Webber. "But when *doesn't* she go out too hard?" He laughed at his own joke.

Maryn detected serious strain in his voice. Pleased about that, she retorted, "It *is* mountain bike racing isn't it?" between gulps of water. The team had just headed out for an early evening training ride on the day after the Elliot Lake race, and while she was grateful for the cooler temperatures of late August, she was still bummed about her loss to Emma—and by only a half bike-length, too. Maryn scowled at the trail ahead. She'd wanted to stay ahead of Emma in the Cup series standings, but now they were tied with three golds and two silvers each as they headed into the Provincial Championships. And now she had Mr. I-Hardly-Train-But-Always-Seem-To-Outride-You on her tail, offering his opinions? *Not helping my mood, Joe. Not at all.*

"Maryn knows what she's doing," Coach Webber said, coming up fast from behind and pedalling abreast of Joe. "She knows that this is an active recovery ride following yesterday's race. She's just settling in to find the best speed. I'm gonna push up ahead to make sure the trail is clear of banana scrapers and death cookies before the rest of the team gets there." He stood up on his pedals and powered off with the ease of a lynx loping lithely up a slight incline.

Maryn admired Coach Webber's muscular legs as he push-pulled away and out of sight. As usual, he sounded just like her dad. Why couldn't they just say "low-hanging branches and rocks that can knock your bike around?" She sighed with envy at his strength and then re-focused her attention on bringing her heart rate down to the level of a proper recovery ride. Joe was still breathing down her neck. She let him pass. This training session was supposed to be about pursuing her own goal—winning the Provincial Championship race next month—and not about staying ahead of her goofy teammate.

Joe pushed on ahead, giving Maryn a few moments of solitude before the main pack came upon her.

"Where's Coach?" asked Charlie, pulling up beside her as if out of nowhere.

"He went up ahead to check out the Hydro Line Loop," Maryn responded.

"I came late and I've been chasing you guys," Charlie said, winded. "What's the drill today? I forgot to check the schedule."

"It's an active recovery ride. Go easy. Just spin your legs out."

"Okay, boss, thanks." Charlie winked at her. "Hey! I hear you're a serious threat to win the big race in September. Only one or two girls in your category can even come close, eh? That one from Newmarket and the new girl from Alberta. That's awesome. Way to go, Maryn." He pulled away in pursuit of their coach.

Maryn nodded and smiled at Charlie's back. She didn't get too worked up about him zooming away from her like that; he had at least three more years of experience than she did, and he trained hard. And despite losing to Emma yesterday, she was definitely proud of her standings in her category. Pedalling on alone again, however, her glum mood returned. The whole Elliot Lake race unfolded in front of her as if she watched it at a movie theatre. She'd taken the lead from the start and had held it for most of the race. Then, on the final loop, less than four hundred metres from the finish, she'd lost her concentration and wobbled dangerously after turning her wheel the wrong way into a loose jumble of rocks. The mistake had only caused a second or two delay, but it had been enough to allow Emma to take over the lead, and Maryn never got it back.

She'd expertly negotiated those rocks on the four previous loops only to screw up when it mattered most, with Emma poised and ready to pounce.

A female voice a few metres behind Maryn jolted her back to the present and made her look back.

"I don't get why we're out here today," whined Stephanie, her face a blotchy red.

"Yeah, I don't get it," echoed Julie. "I mean, isn't it enough that we all busted our humps in Elliot Lake on the weekend? Can't we catch a break? This sucks!"

"Coach designed this workout to *be* a break," Maryn said. "We spin easy to work the lactic acid out of our legs. Active recovery is more effective than just sitting around the day after a race. And anyway," she added with a grin, "what doesn't kill you makes you stronger."

"Yeah, whatever, jock," said Stephanie, rolling her eyes.

Being annoyed can jack up your heart rate too, Maryn thought. This time, she would make her point without words. She pulled away from the complainers, staying a safe distance ahead of them for the rest of the ride.

***

When the team came together again, stretched out on the grass outside the Garage after their ride, Stephanie and Julie continued to grumble about having to train on the Monday after a race weekend. "What's up with this sport, anyway?" snarled Stephanie.

Maryn had been trying to stay patient, but Stephanie's attitude was getting on her nerves. Her anger bubbled up inside her belly. But before she could blow up at her, Coach Webber began to speak.

"Everybody looked great out there," he said.

Maryn glared at Stephanie with her brow furrowed, but then turned her attention back to her coach.

"I know it's not easy to train the day after a race," he said. "You're tired not just from racing but also from travelling. So what I asked the team to do today took dedication and toughness."

Maryn's frustration with Stephanie and Julie evaporated, replaced by pride in her own accomplishment.

"It took physical and mental toughness to make it to this workout," Coach continued. "Just showing up gives you an edge on the competition, and completing it makes you world class."

Stephanie and Julie giggled.

"I mean it," Coach said. "You're training like elite athletes and don't ever forget it."

When Stephanie and Julie rolled their eyes again, Maryn whispered, "Why are you two even doing this if you hate it so much?"

"Duh," Stephanie jeered. "Tight clothes and cute guys sweating in the forest? Why *else* would we be here? Why are *you* here, Maryn? Oh yeah. This is your life. What else could you possibly do? It's in your sad little bike-repair-shop-family veins, isn't it?"

"At least we chose to be here of our own free will," Julie said. "And we aren't Coach Webber wannabees...cuz, like, who'd wanna be?" Both girls laughed and then 'low-fived' one another. Maryn had to use all of her remaining mental toughness to keep herself from punching them.

Just then, Joe distracted Maryn when he sat himself down on the grass beside her. "That's not what I heard," he whispered. "I found out that their parents gave them an ultimatum—choose a team or join a gym. Either way, they were basically ordered to start exercising."

For a short moment, Joe's claim caused Maryn to take pity on the pair. She wouldn't like to be forced to do an extracurricular activity. She believed in pursuing your passion.

"We need to get your bikes cleaned up and put away so you can all get home for a healthy meal and a good night's sleep," Coach said, clapping his hands a couple of times to get everyone's attention. "Our next practice will be on Wednesday for a 7:00 a.m. start. I need to start acclimatizing you to being back at school and training bright and early. Check your schedules ahead of time so you can wrap your heads around the workout before putting your legs into it!" Coach Webber picked up his own water bottle and cycling gloves and walked inside the Garage.

"I guess you weren't the big hot shot you thought you'd be in Elliot Lake," said Julie to Maryn with a smirk. Maryn's sympathy for the girls turned to dust.

"Yeah, you got toasted by that girl from Newmarket." Stephanie scoffed. "Were you doing a *recovery* ride in Elliot Lake?"

"Stephanie, Julie, we're a team." A frowning Coach Webber had come out of the Garage again. "We may compete individually, but we behave as teammates. And teammates support one another, they don't slam somebody when they're down. Understood?"

"Oh, absolutely, Coach," said Stephanie, her face reddening as other team members turned to look at them.

"We were totally kidding, Coach," said Julie.

"I hope so," Coach Webber said. "And I hope you both realize how serious I am about this. I will *not* tolerate cruelty among teammates. It just isn't how we roll here."

Coach immediately turned his attention to helping his youngest athletes deal with getting their gear inside. Stephanie and Julie slithered away in the opposite direction to whisper together by one of the picnic tables.

Maryn pushed her bike onto the concrete slab of the cleaning station and began hosing the dirt off her bike. She could feel the girls' hostile gazes on her as she worked. Coach's defense had likely ticked them off, rather than getting through to them. She fumed but tried to compose herself. Cleaning her bike helped calm her, but didn't stop her hands from shaking. *Tight clothes and cute guys? What the heck? Are these really the kind of people we want on the team?* And what did they know about the Ontario Cup circuit and its ups and downs? Nothing. But, of course, they'd grab any opportunity to try to bring her down a notch.

On the ride home, she chose a seat on the team bus well back from Stephanie and Julie and dropped her backpack on the seat beside her to signal that she needed space. As much as she couldn't stand the sight of them right now, she thought it best to keep them in her range of vision. She didn't trust them. She popped in her earbuds and glared at the huddled duo, not even seeing her beloved forest go by as she seethed silently.

FUMING

Maryn still hadn't recovered from her Stephanie-Julie encounter when she arrived home. She craved the seclusion of her sanctuary, but with everything she had on her plate this evening, she didn't have the time to go there. She entered the breezeway just outside the kitchen to find her mom and Gil boisterously making supper. She did not feel ready to join in, so she took her time unloading her bags while she watched and listened.

"Fuller, why is this chicken still pink in the centre?" her mom called out. She had just cut into a chicken breast with a sharp knife and was now shaking the blade in the direction of her husband with what seemed to be malice.

"Dad was a bit late getting back from the shop, so I started the oven for him," Gil told his mom. "I guess it was later than you said in the note."

"Yes, Gil, but that note was for Dad. *Dad* was supposed to get the chicken going." She shoved the pan back into the oven and banged the door shut, resetting the timer. "He knew that some of us were busy doing stuff until at least seven o'clock this evening, and that we would all be starving by the time everybody got home."

"*You're* starving!" Dad strode into the kitchen and leaned over to kiss his wife. "The kids had snacks, and I ate a late lunch. It's you that's starving."

"Okay fine," said Mom. "But now I have to wait at least 30 minutes before we get to eat and I went to a lot of trouble getting this chicken marinated and ready for a simple button press."

"Here, Darby," Dad said, popping a cracker with cheese and red pepper jelly into her mouth. "This should tide you over until your tasty chicken comes out of the oven. And here's a little something for washing it down." He passed her a glass of Chardonnay. He'd obviously been prepared for her crankiness and had the wine and cheese and crackers ready for her. "Tough day at work?" he asked.

Maryn's mom, who preferred to keep her work-related challenges to herself, shrugged and changed the subject. "What good deed did *you* find yourself doing this afternoon that took you away from our chicken dinner?"

"It was Mr. Martin's slow leak again. I thought we'd patched it and solved the problem, but it seems there was a second tiny hole."

"And, of course, he came at just past closing and you let him in anyway, right?"

"Well, you know, the old fellow walked his bike all the way over from Pine Street..."

"Yes, Fuller, but the man is retired. Why can't he walk the bike over from Pine Street before closing time?"

"Ha! That is indeed the question m'lady," Dad said, bowing like royalty and then grabbing Mom and spinning her around as if they were on a ballroom dance floor rather than their sticky kitchen one.

"You guys are freaks," Maryn said, entering the kitchen. She smiled, but also found herself blinking away tears. They were having so much fun while all she did was practice and work. And it wasn't even September yet. School would just add to her load. She headed toward the stairs and her room. "I'm gonna try to get some piano practicing done before supper."

She had just resumed regular piano practice after taking her summer break. She now had to get her technique and pieces back in shape for when her lessons started up again in the first week of September. Mrs. Landers always held a student recital that month. She liked people to showcase the pieces they'd perfected at the end of the previous school year, preferring not to burden students and their families with a recital in the busy month of June. Now, with September less than two weeks away, panic bubbled up in Maryn.

"Mom, is there anything else I can do to help with supper?" Gil asked.

Maryn stopped on her way up the stairs and mimicked her brother in a little kid voice. "Mom, is there anything else I can do to show you that I'm your most *perfect* child?" Her eyes misted over again.

Gil made a face at her. Her mother said, "Honestly, Maryn, take your issues upstairs along with your muddy clothes."

Maryn stomped upstairs. Her little boy impersonation of Gil wasn't even accurate anymore, because her brother's voice had already changed. How was that possible? He hadn't even gone through a squeaky voice-cracking stage like some of the boys in her grade. He'd just suddenly had a man voice to go along with his man body.

She unloaded her pack, pulling out her smartphone along with her books and lunch bag. Janey had texted her. Maryn responded: *"I have bike, piano, supper #TalkLater?"*

Within seconds, three dots appeared on her screen, indicating that Janey was typing back.

"forgot about your stuff. just watched Degrassi #Lame ttyl"

Reluctantly, because she would have loved nothing more than to flop on her bed and chat with her friend like normal girls her age did, Maryn switched off her lamp and headed out the door to the piano room.

PRACTICE DOES NOT MAKE PERFECT!

Maryn's piece for the recital was a challenging sonata by Haydn that would require serious work. It had a tricky section—a run, like a very fast scale—at the top of page three that kept catching her by surprise.

"Why can't I get this right?" she griped to the empty room. She didn't care that she was talking to herself, even though Gil teased her about it all the time. She was alone. It was Tuesday night, and everyone else was watching TV in the basement rec room, so it wasn't like anyone was going to hear her anyway.

She sipped from her water bottle and then set it on the bench beside her, waiting for the energy drops to kick in and lift some of the fog that seemed to have settled over her brain. She'd stopped using them at the beginning of the summer, but with September looming—along with grade ten, new teachers, the piano recital, and, most importantly, the

Provincial Championships—she'd started up again just to give herself a boost.

She squinted angrily at the page and then played the four-bar section one hand at a time, over and over again at a snail's pace, trying out different fingering options. Then, choosing what she thought was the best one, she penciled the good fingering in above the notes so that she would remember it every time.

She slowly repeated the section with the new fingering, setting the goal of five times without hesitation or error before adjusting her metronome to a slightly faster pace. It was the method she always used to work out the kinks in her pieces. When her dad and brother complained about the grating repetition of the same sections, she responded with, "It may not sound pretty, but it works."

Tonight, however, her method failed. Every repetition of the difficult section was a disaster whenever she tried to increase the pace. Her blood started to boil. Her mind returned to the forest the day before and her encounter with Stephanie and Julie. She had been in school with both of those girls for eleven years and she was tired of the way they always had to be the centre of attention.

"I never wanted any part of *their* stupid clubs," she muttered to herself. "So what are they doing in *my* club now?" Her fingers fumbled the run yet again, and she slammed both fists onto the piano keys, then practically jumped off her bench when her mom knocked and entered the room.

"Somebody seems upset," her mother said. "I wish you wouldn't take your aggravation out on the instrument."

"Sorry, Mom."

"I was just coming to see if you'd like a cup of tea." Mom held out the steaming cup. "It's decaf Earl Grey. But it looks to me like there may be danger of you pitching it against the wall, and this is one of my favourite teacups."

Maryn smiled back at her mother, grateful that she had thought to bring her a cup of tea. "Thanks," she said, sounding appreciative but turning immediately back to her piece.

"You look tired," Mom said, placing the teacup and saucer on the piano just to the right of the keyboard.

"I *am* tired."

"When you're overtired, you get exasperated with your music."

"I know that, but what choice do I have? Mrs. Landers has me playing this piece at the recital, and I'll have to practice for weeks to get it right," Maryn groaned.

"I understand that, Maryn, but practicing should be about quality, not just quantity. Maybe give yourself a break tonight. I'll bet you'd have a much better session tomorrow once you've rested."

"You aren't the one who has to get up to perform for all of those people! You wouldn't dance in front of people unprepared, would you?"

"I'm not suggesting you perform unprepared. Just that you rest and regroup rather than drive yourself and the rest of us crazy up here with your pounding."

Maryn turned her back on her mom, started up the metronome, and resumed playing.

As her mom quietly left the room, hot tears rolled down Maryn's cheeks. Her back hurt. So did her neck and shoulders. She wished her mom had taken her up in her arms and rubbed her back or run her fingers through her hair. She used to do stuff like that. But Maryn knew why her mom hadn't reached out to her. It was because Maryn probably would have pushed her away, yelling, "I'm not a baby. Let me go!"

Sometimes Mom knows me better than I know myself, she thought. She wanted to be independent, and wanted to prove that she was strong. But she was angry a lot of the time. Why did everything have to be so confusing and complicated?

DEVIOUS SCHEME

Maryn surfaced from sleep to the shaking of her bed and the sound of Gil's voice. "Maryn! Time to get up! Dad's already tried to wake you twice. You're going to be late."

She bolted upright, sweat plastering her pajamas to her skin. "How could *they* win?" she wailed.

"How could who win?" Gil asked.

Maryn peered at her bedside clock. Eight o'clock? Seriously? She leapt from the bed, forcing Gil to take a step back. Catching a glimpse of herself in the mirror, she groaned. Why did her hair have to expand every time she slept?

"How could *who* win?" Gil repeated.

"What? N-nobody!" Maryn squeezed her eyes shut, blocking out the dream she'd had of Julie and Stephanie placing ahead of her in a race. She took a deep breath and focused on coming fully awake. It was Monday, she remembered. The second week of school. And—

Her eyes flew open. "Oh no! I meant to get up early to practice before school, and...oh, crap! I didn't finish reading my chapters for English. I'm supposed to hand in the outline for my essay to Mr. Smith today."

"It'll be okay," Gil said.

"How?" she cried.

"If things seem like they're getting out of control, ask for help."

"Oh, come on, Gil. Things don't ever get out of control in your perfect world. So how would you know?"

"Things get out of control plenty in my world. But I can see you're starting to lose it, so I'm trying to help."

"Sorry," Maryn said quietly. As the older of the two, she didn't like Gil to see her heading for a melt down so early in the school year, so she tried to get a grip on her panic.

"You could start by telling Mr. Smith about your Provincial Championships coming up and your recital, and didn't you say that you already have some history thing due...?"

"Argh! I forgot about that. I haven't even started it. I can't talk to Mr. Smith. He'll think I'm asking for special treatment."

"If you don't ask for help, things'll only get worse. Look, if you hurry, you can catch a ride with Mom. She's going to the studio for eight thirty. That way, you can talk to Mr. Smith before the bell." Gil began making Maryn's bed for her as she rifled through her dresser drawers looking for something to wear. "Dad already made your lunch, so just grab something quick to eat in the car."

"Gil, are you seriously making my bed?" Maryn asked.

"Yeah, well, we all step up to the plate sometimes, right?"

"Oh, well, thanks, I guess." She wished she could make herself sound more grateful. But she was too mad about sleeping in.

She got washed up and dressed in record time. Since her family had rallied around her, she got to her first period classroom early. She even took Gil's advice about talking to Mr. Smith.

"Maryn, we need to make arrangements for a few hours to be added to each of your weekdays so you can pack in all of your endeavours and still get some sleep at night," he said, shaking his head in mock seriousness, but smiling at the same time. "If you can get me that outline by tomorrow, that will be fine."

Gil was right again, she thought. She even had extra time to dash to the bathroom before morning announcements.

She yanked her water bottle and energy drops from her back pack. She usually left the drops themselves at home because of Principal Topping's ban on using them on school property, but she hadn't had time to mix them earlier this morning before leaving with her mom. Crouching down, she inspected beneath each of the stall doors to double check that nobody else was in the bathroom with her, then she hurried to one of the sinks to pour some water in her bottle and locked herself into the farthest stall from the bathroom door to mix in the drops.

Her hands shook as she ripped the plastic wrapper from the tiny bottle, partly because she raced the morning bell to get the drink mixed, and partly because she worried about getting caught. *They make rules like that because of people who behave like idiots and put themselves in danger*, Maryn told herself as she squeezed the forbidden liquid into her water. *I'm not like them. I know what I'm doing.*

Two girls burst into the bathroom laughing, their voices identifying them as Stephanie and Julie. They went straight to the sink area, and

Maryn froze part way through mixing her drink. She held her breath, hoping the two girls wouldn't notice she was there. They were talking about Coach Webber.

"Yeah, that should definitely get him off our backs," Stephanie said. "Or, at the very least, it'll keep him busy for a while. I think he deserves it anyway, after humiliating us in front of everybody just because we were teasing his precious superstar."

"Maybe we'll finally be able to quit the team like we want," Julie said. "I can't believe our parents registered us for the fall session without even asking us first!"

"I frigging hate mountain biking. I'd rather pick out my spleen with a shrimp fork than do one more hill repeat," Stephanie complained.

"And the guys on the team are boring," Julie said. "Luckily, my mom was furious when I told her. It took her, like, five seconds to get on the phone and call that club manager Quentin Dorian or whatever his name is. She was like: 'Coach Webber has no business putting his hands on my daughter's bottom!'" Julie chuckled.

"Yeah, my mom bought the story too. But it was my dad who made the call to the club. It was an excellent plan, girlfriend. We should be back to *inactive* recovery by tomorrow."

Maryn's blood seemed to flash freeze in her veins. She kicked open her stall door. "Are you *kidding* me?" She stormed towards the girls, her eyes blazing. "You made up a story about Coach Webber touching your lazy butts just so you could get out of training?"

The two girls stared at Maryn, their mouths agape. The silence spread out between them for what seemed like minutes. But it was really only a few seconds before Stephanie addressed the near apoplectic Maryn.

"That's *exactly* what we did," she said, a gleam in her eyes. "What are *you* gonna do about it?"

"I'm gonna tell everybody it's a lie," Maryn yelled. "I'll tell them I heard you talking about how you made it up."

"Well, here's the thing, Maryn. There're two of us and just one of you, and it's your word against ours," Julie said, wearing an unpleasant grin.

"And look at you standing right here on school property with a banned substance in your hot little hands!" Stephanie pointed at the bottle Maryn had forgotten she held. "A substance our own Principal Topping has told us will result in immediate suspension should it be found in a student's possession. So if you tell anyone what you just heard, we'll report you. You'll get suspended, and I'll get the administration to allow me to post the whole sordid story on the front page of the *Review* for everyone to see. The fall of a hotshot cyclist. Juicy stuff."

"It doesn't matter because what you're saying about Coach isn't true, and nobody'll believe it anyway," Maryn said. "Everybody knows that Coach Webber would never do anything like that."

"Oh, now, that's where you're wrong, cycle chick," Stephanie gloated. "Another coach in the region was caught copping a feel last month, so the bike club has already held an emergency meeting. They've suspended your precious Coach Webber until they can investigate this very serious matter."

The two girls each gave their eye makeup one last check in the mirror before drying their hands and exiting the bathroom, neither of them giving Maryn a second glance.

Maryn remained frozen to the spot, bottles in hand, her breakfast threatening an exit, until the jarring ring of the bell jolted her to action.

HIGH ANXIETY

Math was Maryn's first class that day, and it was awful. Mr. Churchill droned on and on in that nasal voice of his that aggravated her more than usual, and she couldn't stop thinking about her washroom encounter with Stephanie and Julie.

How much trouble would Coach Webber get into because of those two plastics? And what would happen if she got suspended from school? Would Coach decide she wasn't ready for the Canada Cup circuit next season? Would he be so upset with her for ignoring him about the energy drops that he'd kick her off the team? He was really hard on Stephanie and Julie, and that was just for being mean.

She squeezed her eyes shut in an effort to escape the mess she was in. She forced her mind back to a time when the team had held a training camp at Coach Webber and his wife Tommy's cottage. Tommy and

Lydia Bale's mother had also been at the cottage that week along with the team. Maryn remembered feeling thrilled that although she was only eleven years old, Coach had let her go out alone in the rowboat one evening as the sun was setting. Looking back on that time now with older eyes, she realized the lake was pretty small, and Coach and the other chaperones had kept close watch from the shore with a small motor boat handy in case she got into trouble. And of course, they had insisted she wear a life jacket even though she hadn't wanted to.

But from then-Maryn's perspective, she had been alone, floating in the middle of the lake. The air had smelled wonderful, rich with the scent of cedar and berries; and the water swirled as she pulled the oars through the lake's jet-black depths, watching the tiny whirlpools they created.

She remembered how the black of the water had turned to orange with the sunset. She'd pulled the oars out of the water, drops falling silently from them. The rustle and splash of a loon had startled her as it surfaced right beside her boat. He'd been enormous. Their eyes had locked for a moment as they drifted in the quiet. Oh, the astonishing red of his eyes!

She didn't know if it was what he intended, but that evening, Coach Webber had given her the gift of making a deep connection with nature—a connection that had become the way Maryn had cleared her head or resolved her problems ever since. He'd also helped her see she was capable of more than she realized. *He believes in me,* she thought. *And now he might be in huge trouble.*

Her math teacher's voice pulled her back to the present. She knew one thing for sure: she had to find a way to fight for Coach Webber.

***

With her eyes glued to the classroom wall clock for the rest of the morning, school was a write-off. When the clock's hands aligned on twelve at exactly the same moment, Maryn told Janey, who was expecting to eat lunch with her, that she had to do something for her dad and would text her later. Then she ran to the school office and called her father at his shop.

"Dad! We need to talk. It's about Coach."

"Who've you been talking to, Maryn?" His voice sounded tense.

"Those *creeps*, Julie Davis and Stephanie Harwood," Maryn hissed angrily into the phone, trying to keep her voice down so that the office staff could not hear what she was saying.

"Calm down, now."

"I can't calm down! Julie and Stephanie said that the club held some kind of emergency meeting, but they're lying, right?"

"Maryn, we shouldn't talk about this on the phone."

"I know. I want to run over to the bike shop during lunch—which is right now—but I need your permission to go off property. Can you talk to Ms. Dunphy and tell her it's okay for me to leave? Tell her I have a dental appointment or something?"

"Of course. Put her on."

Ms. Dunphy, the office administrator, took the phone from Maryn with a polite smile. As she spoke with Maryn's father, Ms. Dunphy pushed the sign-out sheet in Maryn's direction and tapped on it with her long, authoritative index finger, indicating that Maryn should fill it in. Maryn signed the sheet, then clicked the end of the tethered pen again and again. She jiggled her foot. Ms. Dunphy frowned at her, listening intently to Maryn's father, nodding her head. Maryn needed to get out of there and wanted to scream, "May I *please* go?" Finally, Ms. Dunphy gestured, with a flick of her hand, that she was free to leave.

MAD DASH TO DAD

Maryn sprinted out the school doors in the direction of O'Brien's Bikes. When she ran hard, she could be at the shop in about seven minutes. She'd timed herself many times before. She played this 'race against the clock' game for fun. She logged her times and noted details about footwear, clothing, and health to account for the slight differences in time. But today's race was not for fun.

What about the Provincial Championships? she thought, her panic rising with every step.

"OMG, OMG," she muttered. As she ran, she averted her eyes from the curious gaze of a woman pushing a baby stroller towards her. She wanted to stay calm, but she was bursting with questions. "Dad can straighten this out. I know he can."

But even as she spoke the words, she wasn't certain.

She cut through the alley connecting Sparrow Street to Cardinal Avenue and burst through the door of the bike shop, gulping air and yelling, "Dad? I'm here!" The bells attached to the shop's door signaled her arrival with a clatter and clang. Maryn couldn't help but check the time on her watch. *Six fifty-six—a personal best.*

Then she stopped short. An older couple stood with her dad in front of the kids' bikes. Maryn's eyes grew wide at the thought of having to wait even longer. "Dad?" she said.

"Maryn! This is Mr. and Mrs. Arnold. You know their grandson, Eric. He lives around the corner from us. They're shopping for a trail bike for his birthday. I bet *you* have a recommendation or two," her dad said.

Paralyzed, Maryn said nothing.

The elderly couple nodded with encouragement. "Oh, *yes*," the lady said. "We would *love* to hear what you recommend. We hear you've been a bike aficionado for many years."

"Oh, um, yeah, I guess so," Maryn said, snapping out of her paralysis and trying to catch her breath. "I was a big fan of the Trek Superfly 20 when I was Eric's age." She walked over to the bike in question. "In my opinion, it's still the best today, especially if he's a boy who likes to go off road and stir up some dirt."

She tried smiling, but as she forced her mouth to curve upwards, she felt like she was channelling Johnny Depp's version of the Mad Hatter in the movie Alice in Wonderland. Her dad seemed to think the same thing, because he shuffled her off into the back room. "Look, I'm sorry, Sprint, but I've gotta finish up here before we can talk," he whispered. "Why don't you take this box cutter and open a few of those boxes while I deal with the Arnolds, okay?"

"Dad. My lunch break is over in another thirty minutes. I...I..."

"Maryn." He placed both his hands on her shoulders and lowered his head to stare into her eyes, his gaze calm and reassuring. "Open the boxes. Hold it together."

The lava bubbling inside Maryn slowed to a gentle simmer. She took a deep breath and nodded.

"I can do that."

Maryn began slicing the shipper tape on the tops of several cardboard boxes, opening through one after another. Moving from box to box, she recalled how Coach calmed her down if she panicked during training. He reminded her about her short-term and long-term goals. *"Maryn, you've set serious goals. But I let you set them because I knew you could meet them head-on. You've got determination, ambition and the work ethic to back it all up, and I'll be here to guide you through."*

But he won't be here, she thought. She pulled a small cycling jersey out of one of the boxes. She held it up. Her heart sank. "What can *I* do to help Coach?" she muttered under her breath. "Especially with Stephanie and Julie threatening me!" She brushed a tear from her cheek. The shop door's bells signaled the departure of the Arnolds.

SUSPENSION SHOCKER

Maryn emerged from the back room, utility knife in hand. She watched her father while he finished up at the till. He reached out to take her knife. He looked different. Tired and sad.

"Dad?" For a moment, she was a little girl again, thinking, *Dad will make everything all right.* But this wasn't a scrape on her knee. This was big. Things were a long way from all right.

"Okay, let's start with what you know." Dad's tone was business-like. "Tell me everything, and we'll go from there."

In an explosion of strong words, Maryn recounted part of the scene in the girls' restroom, holding back the part about the energy drops and their threats to expose her. She told him she'd overheard Stephanie and Julie talking about Coach's suspension, and that they claimed they'd been touched on 'the bottom' by him. Her indignation and frustration began to build as she shared her story. "They can't get away with this, can they? Nobody actually believes this stuff, do they? What are the board members saying? What happened at the meeting?"

"Okay, Maryn. The first question I have to ask—because I care about you more than words could ever convey—is if you've ever felt uncomfortable around Coach Webber. Has he ever touched you inappropriately?"

"Ohmigod, Dad, no! Are you kidding me? You're Coach's best friend! How could you think that...even for a second?"

Maryn could no longer hold back her tears. They poured in sheets down her hot cheeks.

Dad opened his long arms wide to wrap them around her shaking shoulders. She cried as he held her tight and murmured, "I know. This is awful. But you know what?"

"What?" Maryn asked in a muffled voice, her breaths short, staccato inhalations. Her dad stepped back. He held her shoulders and looked directly into her eyes. "If Coach has done nothing wrong, then the truth will prevail."

"Dad? Has he really been told to stop coaching while the board investigates?"

"Yes. The board was obliged to suspend him temporarily while they look into this. It was the responsible thing to do."

"Responsible! It's over-the-top. Coach didn't do anything wrong. I'm sure of it." The rest of the conversation with Stephanie and Julie nagged at Maryn, but again she held it back, wanting to believe—needing to believe—that Coach would be okay without her having to admit to everything. She wiped her nose with the back of her hand. "What will happen while he's under suspension? Who'll coach the team?

Who'll help us prepare for the Provincial Championships?"

"We're hopeful that this will blow over before we know it. In the mean time, the board is still trying to sort that out."

"This is so unfair!" Maryn stood scowling, breathing heavily. She considered telling her dad the truth about what Stephanie and Julie had said. But she was scared, thinking about being suspended from school, kicked off the bike team and dragged through the mud in the school newspaper. Maybe Dad was right. Maybe this would blow over quickly.

"Listen, it's time for you to get back to school. We can talk about this some more this evening."

Maryn's feet seemed stuck to the shop floor. Once she left the safety of this room with its comforting aroma of tire rubber and bike chain grease, things would get a lot tougher. "Dad?"

"Yes?"

"What can I do to help?"

"Nothing, Sprint," he said. "This is in the hands of the adults now."

Maryn considered his answer for a moment, then frowned. No. She stomped her right foot, shaking herself from her paralysis. No way would she sit back and do nothing. Not when Coach was in this much trouble. She turned and charged out the door, vowing over her shoulder, "I'm going to do something!"

EVERYTHING SUCKS!

Maryn dashed off again immediately after school that day. She grabbed her things from her locker, apologized to Janey, and headed straight to her mom's dance studio. Mom would be teaching until six thirty, and she couldn't wait until then to see her.

This time, she had to take a city bus. It was jammed with high school students and a smaller population of adults heading home from work. Maryn tried doing the reading for Mr. Smith's outline, but her mind kept wandering to the bathroom conversation and her talk afterward with her dad. How would she be able to help Coach if she couldn't divulge what Stephanie and Julie had said?

She searched the faces of the other bus riders, looking for signs that they might feel miserable too. But only smiling, giggling people surrounded her, chatting with their fellow passengers as if nothing was wrong. *Wake up and smell the coffee, people!* she screamed inside her head. *Everything sucks!*

The bus braked hard at that precise moment and the resulting high-pitched screech of its brake pads created a perfect synchronicity with Maryn's private thoughts. She stood up on her tiptoes to see why the bus driver had slammed on his brakes. A young boy of six or seven had followed a tennis ball from his yard into the path of the bus, and now his mother and the bus driver were both taking him to task about it as his mother held him in her arms just outside the bus door. Both adults wagged their fingers at him, and he hid his face in his mom's chest.

Maryn's temporarily icy heart melted at the sight of the boy being chastised. She felt his fear and embarrassment as if they were her own.

After two more stops, she rang the bell, muttered an apology as she squeezed past the woman seated next to her on the aisle, and exited swiftly out the side door. A brisk two-block jog later, she stood at the foot of the stairs at the Darby O'Brien School of Dance. She entered the main door and checked the clock in the hallway. It was five minutes past four, which meant her mom had ten more minutes with the kindergarten dancers. With back-to-back classes scheduled, she would only have a moment to talk.

Maryn peeked through the small pane of glass in the door. She watched her mother's shoulders beneath the thin straps of a pale blue leotard, taking comfort in the unyielding arm position and the power locked up in the long, lean muscles.

Her mother demonstrated a slow turn for her small charges and in so doing, caught Maryn's eye through the tiny window. Within twenty seconds, she had the tiny dancers seated on the floor doing a stretching exercise while she excused herself. She opened the door of the studio, pulled Maryn inside and herded her up a short staircase to a backstage area away from the ten sets of eyes below.

There she turned her daughter to face her. "Oh sweetie," she said. "Dad told me you know about Coach Webber being under investigation."

"And suspended!" Maryn moaned. Her eyes filled with tears.

"It'll be really tough training without your coach with the big race coming up this weekend," Mom said. "And it'll be tough on Coach too. This is a *very* unfortunate situation."

Maryn watched her mom's face, hoping for a sign that things would get better soon. As if she'd read her thoughts, Mom's expression saddened.

"I have no real words of comfort to share with you at this point, Maryn. But Dad and I will get an update from the board early this evening. We'll keep you informed. The best we can all do is stay strong and positive."

"But how?"

"By taking everything Coach has taught you and putting it into practice. Remember the path you're on. Keep your goals in mind. Stay focused. Keep working hard. That's what Coach would want you to do."

"That's true."

"Do you want to stay here at the studio and do your homework until I'm finished teaching? You can even set up in here if you'd like."

Maryn nodded silently. She had a lot of work to do and it would feel good to stay close to her mom.

When her mother left to resume teaching, Maryn reached into her bag and felt around for her books. Her hand brushed against the cool metal of her water bottle and the little bottle of energy drops still wrapped in paper towel from the school bathroom. She pulled both items out of her bag and held them up in front of her, carefully considering what their contents meant to her. She stifled the desire to throw them both against the studio wall. Then, overcome with exhaustion, she popped the lid off the water bottle, squeezed in the remaining energy drops, and then swallowed the whole concoction as if she had been deprived of fluids for days. *I might as well benefit from something in this whole crappy situation,* she thought, feeling both reckless and ashamed at the same time.

GAG ORDER

Maryn was battling with the sonata before supper, a freshly-mixed bottle of energy drink by her side, when her parents knocked and entered the room.

"Sorry to interrupt, Maryn, but we have something important to tell you about the situation with Coach Webber," her dad said, pulling the plastic chair up close to her piano bench, turning it around backwards and straddling it. To Maryn, he seemed too relaxed to be addressing the Coach situation. Her mom sat a bit further away on the loveseat against the wall. The room seemed crowded.

Maryn slowly turned herself around on the bench to face her parents. "Unless you're here to tell me that the board has figured out that those morons are lying and that everything'll be back to normal tomorrow, then I'm not sure I wanna hear about it."

"We would all love for this to be over, but that is *not* the case," her mom said quietly. "Yet."

"The board is very concerned about containing the situation for Coach Webber's sake," Maryn's dad said.

"Containing the situation?"

"Yes. Keeping the complaint a secret, except from the people who are directly involved in the investigation."

"Sometimes even when a complaint of this nature ends up being false," Mom explained, "The accused is forever tainted by it. Even if you never did a bad thing to anyone, an incident like this can follow you around for life."

"We want to avoid that happening to Coach," Dad said. "So the six members of the board have agreed they will not say a word about this allegation while the investigation is still going on."

"Do the other athletes know?"

"No, they do not," her dad said. "And Stephanie and Julie were asked not to speak of this until the investigation has been completed."

"But they've already spoken about it at school."

"That's right. Even though they thought they were alone in the school restroom, they still broke the rules of the agreement, and the board is aware of that. I told Pia on the phone this afternoon."

"What? You told Ms. Bianchi?"

"Maryn, we've *got* to get a handle on this, for Coach's sake. And we're going to start with us."

"What does that mean?"

"It means we're going to make it a house rule—a *family* rule—to only talk about this under controlled circumstances."

"I don't get it." Maryn frowned.

"We mean that we will not talk about the situation with Coach Webber outside of our house," Dad said. "Not even if it's just the four of us."

"Does Gil know what's going on?"

"Yes, we told Gil the basics. We kept to the facts as we know them, and told him we'll update him as things develop. But otherwise, this will not be a topic of conversation anywhere—not even at our own dinner table."

"Why?"

"Because practicing *not* talking about it begins at home," her mom said. "If it's a regular topic at dinner, it may slip out in public. And that can only hurt Coach Webber."

"Understood?" her dad asked.

"Understood." Maryn lowered her head and spun herself around to face the keyboard with a sigh.

"And that includes Janey, okay?"

Maryn glared back over her shoulder at her dad. She had planned on giving Janey the whole run down later that evening. Her friend would totally understand what she'd been through. But she knew her parents would not bend on this point. "Okay," she said. How would she ever keep that promise?

Her parents exchanged a concerned glance.

"Maryn, we're not saying you can't come to us privately with questions about this. Or if something is bothering you, you can certainly talk to us about it," Dad said. "We just don't want it to be regular suppertime conversation. Do you see the difference?"

"I think so."

"Okay then." Her dad patted her on the back as he stood up. He grabbed his chair and returned it to its corner.

"Ten minutes until supper, honey," Mom said, following him from the room.

Maryn was about to start playing again when she heard her parents talking quietly in the hallway.

"I've known Loman Webber my whole life," Dad said. "He is simply *not* capable of doing something like this."

"I absolutely agree."

"But if Loman is innocent, that means those girls are lying. And what would ever possess them to do such a thing?"

"Good question. In any event, serious allegations warrant serious action. Everyone needs to go through the process of properly investigating the situation. It will be the only way to restore Loman's good name and protect the club's reputation. Maybe this is just some kind of teen girl drama, but when those girls train with the team, they're under the club's care. Pia Bianchi and the board are doing the right thing looking out for them and for the other athletes. I just feel terrible for Loman and Tommy. What a nightmare."

Her parents' fading footfalls marked their departure, and Maryn tried to resume her practice. She peered at the notes on the page through hazy eyes. It was as if this section of the piece was somehow related to the whole mess with Coach...like it couldn't be fixed until Coach's situation was, too. She tried to play it again and got caught up—fingers tangled, hesitations glaring, and errors blaring. It was hopeless. How would she be able to perform this piece at the recital when parts of it seemed as impossible to solve as the situation with Coach? And how could she help solve that problem without telling everyone about Stephanie's and Julie's lie and exposing herself in the process?

SUBSTITUTE COACH

"Maryn, time to get up for training," her dad said, shaking her gently.

Maryn opened one eye and squinted at the clock on her bedside table. It was 5:45 a.m. on Wednesday. At this time of year, it was dark outside, but she still had to eat breakfast, put together a post-training snack and a lunch for school, and pack her school clothes before leaving the house.

She sat up and, as was her daily ritual, inspected the race countdown calendar. The Provincial Championships were only four days away. But there was more. Wearily, she regarded her recent hand-written note on the same date: Piano Recital. Mrs. Landers had scheduled the piano recital for 4:00 p.m. on the same day as her final Ontario Cup race of the season.

Epic, she thought.

"Will Coach be there this morning?" she asked her dad, hopefully.

"No, he won't. The board has asked me to lead as many of the scheduled practices as I can for a little while, with Charlie Gibson's help."

Maryn nodded. She threw her legs over the side of the bed. She had woken up momentarily forgetting about the situation with Coach. But now her heart plummeted as it all came back, one depressing detail at a time.

"The team has been told that Coach had to take a temporary leave of absence to attend to a family matter," her dad added.

"What about Stephanie and Julie? Will they be at practice?"

"Their parents have said they're not ready to entrust their children to anybody connected with the club."

"Really." Maryn used a tone that sounded more annoyed than relieved. "So I guess those two got their wish."

"What do you mean?" Her dad stopped part way to her bedroom door and turned back, confusion visible in his eyes.

Maryn stared back at him. Once again, she considered telling the truth about what she had witnessed in the bathroom, but Stephanie and Julie's words rang loudly in her head: *"We'll report you...You'll get suspended...We'll post the whole sordid story in the Review!"*

Reminding herself of her dad's words, *"We're hopeful that this will blow over before we know it,"* she decided once again to keep the truth to herself. She changed the subject.

"So you're my coach now." Her demeanor would have been the same if she'd announced that a transport truck had run over her bike. "I have a pretty big race this weekend, you know."

"It'll be like old times, Sprint."

Maryn peered at her father with a downcast expression.

"We'll stick to the plan, okay?" he encouraged cheerfully. "Every step we take will be exactly the way you and Coach mapped it out."

She stood, sighed, and then pulled some clothes out of her closet for the day ahead.

***

Maryn sat in silence in her dad's truck all the way to the Garage parking lot where everybody would meet to start the ride. Drained and worried about tackling her training, she'd squirted a stream of energy drops into her water at home. She took a sip from her bottle now in preparation.

Their workout today would be relatively short and would take just forty-five minutes to complete. Afterward, the team bus would pick the kids up outside the Garage and deliver each cyclist/student to one of the many schools attended by team members.

"Okay, gang," Dad said, smiling at the group standing in front of him, geared up and ready to go. "I'm Fuller O'Brien. Some of you know me as Maryn's dad. As your parents may have already told you, Coach Webber will be missing a few practices. So, for the time being, Charlie and I will be taking the lead."

"How long will Coach be away?" Joe asked.

"We're hoping he'll be back in no time. But we can't say for sure at this point."

"What's the plan for the workout?" Maryn asked, impatient to start.

"Charlie?" Her dad gestured for the eighteen-year-old to take over, giving him the opportunity to brief the team.

"We'll start with a couple of flat loops around the dam—spinning in an easy gear to warm up—then we'll do some light hill repeats," Charlie said. As some of the cyclists groaned, he added, "Nothing too strenuous. The hill we've chosen isn't much of a hill at all. But it'll keep your muscles ready for tackling hills. We want you to stay sharp for Sunday's race. We'll allow thirty minutes for the main set of hill repeats, so just do as many as you can accomplish in that time."

With twenty-eight athletes in attendance, there would be just enough time for everybody to clean and lock up their bikes and have a quick shower before getting on the bus. The schools had different start times, so the bus driver planned the route accordingly.

Maryn was ready to get riding. Charlie had barely finished talking when she took off. She just wanted to be on her bike where everything always made more sense. She was also eager to feel a little burn in her leg muscles.

"Easy peasy, right, Maryn?" her dad said with a wink as he and Charlie passed her two minutes later, accompanied by the silky whoosh of briskly turning wheels. Maryn had to breathe deeply to control the anger rising within her as the two of them sailed off ahead and out of sight. She grabbed her water bottle and took a big gulp, feeling her heart rate rise when she did. Was it because of the energy drops, or because of her frustration at watching them whirl away from her?

She reminded herself that this kind of competitive frustration was a waste of energy—something she should channel instead into her training session. And so, with a couple of deep breaths, she willed her negative feelings to dissolve and transformed them into a solid confidence as she flew through the flat section of the course. Even the cool wind seemed to sing her praises.

"You are strong and swift," it cheered, and Maryn soon felt as if she and her bike were a single instrument of strength and speed.

"Hey Maryn!" a voice called out from behind, startling her. It was

Joe. She didn't answer, trying to stay focused on what she was doing, but oblivious as usual, Joe continued talking. "Have you gotten very far on that history thing for Ms. Price?"

Maryn did not want to talk about the assignment. "I'm doing okay," she said flatly, trying to shut Joe down and stay on track with her workout. In truth, she had barely started doing the research.

"I wonder why Stephanie and Julie puppied out and missed training this morning?" Joe mused.

Maryn shrugged.

"You'd think they'd be hyped about getting to race at the Provincial Championships. Even though they'll just be racing as beginners, it'll still be a sweet thing for them to be a part of."

Maryn's breathing had turned to wheezing. She slammed her bike into a higher gear, charging ahead of Joe with a surge of speed that was definitely not part of her training plan. *I've got to get away from this conversation,* she thought.

Her heart rate skyrocketed. In her mind, her mom's voice cautioned her to calm down. *"Maryn, don't get yourself into a state."* A series of images flashed through her brain: one of her eating Emma Sutcliffe's dust at the Provincial Championships; another where she messed up the doomed section of the sonata during her performance at the recital; and finally, one where she hadn't even started her history assignment by the due date.

"Arghh!" Maryn snarled to the trees, the birds, and anything else in her path. "This is all wrong!" Coach had taught her all about visualization. She needed to visualize *success* not failure...to picture her victorious race on Sunday, her masterful piano performance at the recital, and the completion of her history project on time.

And the proper completion of this workout was a step in the direction of that success. She slowed herself back down to finish warming up at the correct pace. Then she tackled the hill repeats just as Charlie and her dad had instructed.

"One positive step at a time," she told herself, echoing Coach's mantra and feeling a thousand times better.

EMPTY THREATS

Maryn opened the door to her classroom with clammy hands. She dreaded facing Stephanie and Julie. She, Joe, and Charlie had been the last cyclists dropped off at school, arriving shortly after morning announcements. She carried a late slip to give to Mr. Smith, but it wasn't her teacher she worried about.

"Here you are, Maryn," Mr. Smith said, his jovial tone indicating good humour. "How was your early morning ride?"

Maryn caught Stephanie's eye before looking back at Mr. Smith and answering with a simple, "Good." Then she set her backpack on his desk and dug out her essay outline. She had completed it after practicing piano the night before. "Here," she said, holding out her outline without further explanation.

"Ah, yes, thanks Maryn," He took the paper from her and nodded.

"As agreed."

Stephanie's eyes followed Maryn, and when Maryn reached the side of her desk, the other girl asked in a clear voice, "How's your *energy* this morning, Maryn?"

Julie, one row over, cracked up.

Maryn ignored both of them and sat down as quietly as she could. She had interrupted the start of Mr. Smith's class and didn't want to delay his lesson further. Janey gave Maryn a funny look and nodded her head towards Stephanie and Julie as if to say, "What's with those two?" But Maryn just shrugged and took out her books.

"Stephanie, Julie, I'll thank you to socialize *after* class," said Mr. Smith. "Right now, I want you to turn your attention back to the thirteenth page of the Edgar Allan Poe story. Julie, why don't you start us off by reading the next few pages out loud?"

Maryn tried to concentrate on the words Poe had written, but she found that none of them made any sense today. Normally, she would have taken out her water bottle by now. She'd been keeping it on her desk throughout the school day over the past couple of weeks, already mixed with the energy drops. But today, she kept it hidden away in her bag. Stephanie and Julie would be watching her closely, and if they spotted the bottle, they might broadcast her illicit behaviour to everyone in the class.

Julie's voice bubbled away, reading the story. *Leave it to Julie to make Edgar Allan Poe sound like an article from a teen magazine,* Maryn thought.

Stephanie turned slightly toward Maryn. "Make sure you look at the *Review*'s most recent post, jock," she hissed, her smile menacing. "I was recently inspired to launch an exposé on this whole scandal about the abuse of energy drops by high school students."

Maryn gave her a dirty look. She wanted to say that nothing her lame high school newspaper posted would ever be of interest to her, but she did not want to make Mr. Smith angry.

Maryn worried that Stephanie had implicated her in the energy drop abuse story. Her heart raced, just as it had during her ride earlier that morning, making her feel the way she imagined that lost ferret had felt when her neighbour's dog had cornered it in their back yard. But when Mr. Smith asked a question about the text Julie had read, Maryn answered it confidently.

She was a good student, she reminded herself. She was a good person. She wasn't doing anything wrong. She was just having trouble staying awake long enough to get all of her work done, and she was having problems getting through her training sessions without a boost. That didn't make her part of an abuse scandal. *I'll clear Coach's name and show everyone that those two are liars.*

But how could she do it without getting herself into hot water?

∗∗∗

At lunch, Maryn and Janey sat together on a bench outside, reading Stephanie's article on their phones.

"Well, it's not exactly an *exposé*, is it?" Maryn scoffed.

"Did she *call* it an exposé?" Janey asked.

"Yeah, she did."

"Hm. Well, to me, it's just an ordinary story about the kids at Maple Grove High School and what happened to them when they played that ridiculous game with the energy drops. The same story was already covered in the Redford newspaper."

"You're right."

"They *do* make a connection to our school by writing about Principal

Topping's suspension policy after the Maple Grove students ended up in the hospital," Janey observed.

"Right."

"I actually wish they'd provided more information about the health problems these drops can cause. Wouldn't *you* be interested in that?"

"I guess."

"Are you still using them?"

"Yeah," Maryn said softly.

"Be careful. I'm worried about you. You don't seem yourself. Is there something going on that you aren't telling me?"

Janey knew her so well. She longed to tell her everything. "Yes. There's something going on, but my parents won't let me talk about it."

"What?" Janey sucked in a quick breath.

Maryn shook her head. "I *really* want to tell you what's going on. But I'm scared that if I don't listen to my parents, it might make things worse."

"Oh," Janey said, her forehead puckered in a frown. She kept quiet for long moment. Finally, when she spoke again, she was her usual, supportive self. "Okay, Maryn, don't tell me. Listen to your parents."

"Thanks. You're the best."

"Just remember, I'm here if you need me."

***

Maryn headed straight for her sanctuary after school. It'd been way too long since she'd been there. She paced along the edge of the trail waiting for a break in the stream of students and adults who walked home from school or work that way. At last, with nobody in sight, she scooched through the dense brush, catching her sleeve and scratching her shins on sharp thorns and shoots as she pushed forward in more haste than usual.

The maple grove's open air caressed her face the moment she escaped the clutches of the underbrush. She paused, breathing in the sweet smell of moss and damp earth, then dropped to the sun-dappled forest floor. Gazing up at the gigantic maples towering over her, she imagined that she could draw some of their great strength into her bones. The river beyond whispered assurances that she could—and would—hatch a plan to save Coach. Slowly, the tension drained from her as the forest wrapped her in a warm hug. It held her until she felt ready to leave...ready to carry out the plan she'd come up with. She whispered her thanks as she left.

HATCHED PLAN

Maryn sat poised, erect, like a lioness staking out her prey. Mom and Dad were both still at work, and she worked on her history assignment in her bedroom, keeping an eye on the clock, impatiently counting the minutes as she waited for Gil to get home from his batting practice.

When the telltale thump of the side door signaled Gil's arrival, she pushed aside her laptop and bolted to her bedroom door to get ready for the ambush. Gil would be upstairs within seconds. He always carried his backpack up to his room and changed out of his baseball uniform before he did anything else. Today, his unfailing punctuality and routine filled Maryn with gratitude. As he began walking past her door, she jumped out, pulled him into her room, and slammed the door.

He staggered, caught himself, and stared at her. "Maryn—what the heck?"

"Shush, Gil, just a second," Maryn ran over to her window to check for her mom's car or her dad's bike, just in case she'd missed their arrival. "I have to talk to you about something, and Mom and Dad can't know that we're having this conversation."

"Okay, I guess. What's up?" Her brother plopped himself down on her bed, setting his pack at his feet. He pulled off his ball cap and messed with his shiny black hair, trying to get it to return to its normal state. But his ordinarily poker-straight hair had curled a bit from him sweating, and the ball cap had imprinted a ring on it.

"I know we're not supposed to talk about this Coach stuff," Maryn said, pacing back and forth beside her bed, "but I can't stand it any-more. I have to do something. I can't just sit back and let a bunch of adults 'investigate' while the whole team goes without a coach."

"Aren't Dad and Charlie taking over the coaching for now?"

"That's not good enough!" Maryn lunged again towards her win-dow to scan the property for parents. "I need him back. The whole team needs him back. We have the Provincial Championships this weekend." Her voice rose with each word. "You know how much that race means to me—it's where Coach is supposed to decide when I can join the Canada Cup circuit."

As she spoke, her voice shook along with the rest of her body. Darn it! It must be the drops getting to her; she'd been taking them all day.

"Okay, I get that." Gil used his cool-headed voice, the one that usu-ally got Maryn even more riled up. "But what's your plan?"

"I was thinking that we should create a list of all the great things Coach has been involved in. You know, things for kids like training camps, workshops, charity rides and stuff like that."

"Yeah?" Gil said, turning his hand in little circles, motioning for her to go on.

"I figure we could contact all of those kids and get them to come forward to say what a great guy Coach is, and that he has never done anything to hurt them. People might not believe just me, but they might believe an army of kids!"

"But this whole thing is supposed to be kept secret. Nobody is supposed to know that an investigation is taking place."

"But how are these *investigators* doing it? How can they investigate without having to explain what's going on?"

Gil frowned and said, "I don't know." He eyed himself in the mirror above her dresser, running his fingers through his hair in another failed attempt to repair his hat-head. "I guess investigators know how to talk about stuff without letting on what they're really talking about. Like on TV when they can kind of trick people into telling them things."

"This is ridiculous. It's a ridiculous waste of time. If we could get a bunch of kids to come forward and say—all together—that Coach is the greatest, it would help prove he's innocent. If each kid said, 'He worked with me on this, that and the other thing and he never, ever, *ever* did anything bad,' then wouldn't this whole thing just go away?"

"I don't know...you've got to be really careful with stuff like this."

"But I want to jump up and down in front of that stupid board and scream at the top of my lungs—with all the kids he ever coached—and make them *see*."

Gil jabbed at his pack with one foot, shaking his head. "Mom and Dad are smart. They usually know what's best, and they said to keep quiet for now."

"Damn!" Maryn glared at her brother. "I knew you'd say that!"

"Well...if you knew, then why'd you pull me in here?"

"I was hoping you'd help me create the list and get hold of the kids. You and I know a lot of them from school and from so many years on the team. And we both know people who use the Garage and bike trails for cross-country skiing in the winter."

"Oh, yeah. But I still think you should run your plan past Mom and Dad."

"You know what they'll say."

"Yeah, they'll probably say no because they said we had to let adults handle this." He stood and picked up his pack by one strap, slinging it over his right shoulder. "Your plan doesn't sound like a bad one, really. It just might not be time yet, and I don't think we should mess with this on our own."

Hearing Gil say it wasn't a bad plan calmed Maryn down. She stopped pacing for a moment, unsure what to say next. A thump at the side door sent her back to the window, where she spied their dad's bike parked in its usual spot. She had to wrap this conversation up quickly.

"Maryn! Gil!" their dad called from downstairs.

"Maryn," Gil said. "I promise I'll help you with this if Mom and Dad agree to it. If they say it's a good plan, we'll do it, okay? We'll work hard and we'll get those kids together. But we need to know from Mom and Dad that this is all right. We don't want to do anything that could hurt Coach's career, right?"

"Right." Her energy-drop fueled body still wanted to go, go, go. But maybe Gil was right. Maybe they should wait. She shivered a little as she shifted down from 'go' to 'slow,' which wasn't a gear she was accustomed to using. She breathed in deeply, then reached a state of cool resolve.

"Okay." She nodded. "Let's talk to Mom and Dad."

DASHED HOPES

"Gil, you grate the carrots for the salad while Maryn scrambles the eggs," Dad said, tossing a bag of carrots over Maryn's head and into his son's hands.

"Is it egg night again already?" Maryn asked. The family had mutually decided that they deserved one night a week where dinner was quick and uncomplicated...unlike their various schedules. So eggs had become the go-to quick meal on Wednesdays.

"Egg night already, Sprint," her father answered.

"When will Mom be home?" She and Gil had agreed not to talk about her idea until both parents were home.

Dad glanced up at the wall clock as he grabbed a pile of plates from the cupboard. "I'd say five minutes," he replied. "The broccoli is ready for steaming. How's that salad coming, Gil? Do you want the spinner for the romaine?" He took the device from a shelf in the pantry even as he asked.

"Should I put some cheese in with the eggs?" Maryn asked as she poured the raw scrambled eggs into a pan on the stove.

"Good idea." Her dad opened the fridge in search of a chunk of cheddar. "Are you finished with the grater, Gil?"

"Yep, I'm on to peppers."

Dad took the grater from him and swept away a few carrot bits with his fingers before grating the cheese into Maryn's panful of eggs.

"Does anyone want me to put on some music?" he asked. But the clunk of a car door and the click of shoes coming up the walk caused Maryn to respond abruptly.

"No, Dad. No music, okay?"

"Have you got a headache?" He reached across the island counter-top to feel her forehead.

"No. I...we just have something we need to talk about now that Mom's home." Maryn stirred the eggs to keep them from sticking to the pan.

"Hi everyone." Mom called out in a singsong voice from the side door. She poked her head into the kitchen and smiled. "It's nice to see you all working together like this. Yum. Egg night!"

"We're almost ready to get it all on the table, Darby. Can you eat right away?" Dad asked.

"Always!"

Oh boy, Maryn thought. *They're both in such great moods. I hate to wreck that.* But time was of the essence because Mom had to go back to work in less than an hour. Her dad was already doling out huge portions of steamed broccoli.

"Bring the eggs over, Maryn," he said. "Gil, let's have that salad over here too."

"Uh, Dad? Mom?" Maryn turned off the burner beneath the eggs. "I know we made a house rule not to talk about the Coach thing at home, and you said it couldn't be dinner conversation, but I have something I need to talk to you about. I need both of you to hear this. And Mom has to leave soon. So can we break the rule this evening? Just this once?"

"Of course," her dad said after making eye contact with her mom and getting an affirmative nod.

"Maryn, the rule was put in place to reduce the risk of one of us spilling the beans outside of the house," Mom said. "But if you've got something important to discuss, and the only time we have all together is suppertime, then there's no problem."

Mom, Maryn, and Gil sat down at the kitchen table while Dad filled everyone's water glasses. Then he sat too, focused his attention on Maryn, and said: "Okay. What's up?"

Since talking her plan through with Gil, Maryn was composed and more determined. It helped knowing that Gil also believed it was a good plan. She used the techniques Coach Webber had taught her to focus her attention on her goal—this time to convince her parents that her plan was a possible solution.

They listened without interruption as Maryn spoke. To her surprise, they did not look agitated or upset by her proposal. Gil also listened intently, letting her do all the talking, but nodding his head in agreement as she presented each point. Once she had finished, Maryn found herself staring at the rest of her family. It was a rare moment of quiet at the O'Brien supper table.

"The team needs Coach back," she urged, unable to stand the silence any longer. "Think about everything he's done over the years—teaching, coaching and advising kids—I want to be the one to pull those kids together to speak up for him. Gil's offered to help contact everyone."

Her parents looked at one another, and then Mom signaled for Dad to respond because she still had an entire plate of food to consume before work. As she scooped up eggs, gently stabbed broccoli florets, and chewed, Dad cleared his throat.

"Maryn, we think it's great that you've put so much thought into this," he began. Maryn looked at Gil and raised one eyebrow, unsure where this was going as Dad continued, "This is something that the board has talked about as well. On the surface, it seems like an excellent idea."

"On the surface?" Maryn challenged, her throat tightening as she held back the threat of tears.

"Yes." Dad put down his fork to use his hands for the explanation that was to come. "One of the board members is a lawyer with some experience in this area. She explained to us that presenting a list of all of the activities Coach has done with kids over the years can actually be detrimental to him."

"Detrimental? How can a bunch of kids saying how great Coach is and how much he's helped them be a *bad* thing?" Maryn banged her glass down on the table.

"I know, I know, Maryn. We wondered the same thing at first. But this woman explained that a long list of involvement with children could make it look like Coach has been planning this—that he's been working with kids over the years to put himself in a position to do them harm." Dad used his napkin to wipe condensation from his glass.

"But if the kids say that he did no harm, then that changes everything, doesn't it?"

"Well, here's the thing," her dad said, placing his hand over hers. "We're trying to keep this from going public. We're hoping that this whole thing will be shut down and put to bed even before it starts."

"But how? What are the investigators *doing*?"

"The police are talking to Coach; they're talking to the girls who've made these accusations; and they're examining Coach's home computer, laptop, and phone—things that Coach willingly surrendered to them."

Maryn met her dad's gaze, letting him keep his hand on hers. Mom, who had finished eating, took a long drink of water and joined in the conversation.

"Maryn, if Coach gets charged with inappropriately touching these girls, then *that* is the point at which your plan could go into effect," she said. "If this goes to trial, Coach will need all of the organizations and kids he has helped to come together and speak on his behalf. But we're hoping he will never be charged, that this won't go to trial, and that nobody ever has to come forward to defend him."

"Do you have any idea how things are going?" Maryn asked.

"No. We're letting the investigators do their thing," Dad said.

"Well, how long is 'their thing' going to take? It feels like this has been going on forever."

"I know, sweetie," Mom said. "But it's only been a couple of days. We all feel the same way."

"No, we *don't* all feel the same way!" Maryn pulled her hand out from beneath her dad's hand. She pushed back her chair and jumped up to glare at her mom. "Because we haven't *all* lost our coach before a big race. My most important race. I had a plan to *do* something. I thought we could work together to get Coach back, and I thought we could start right after supper. Gil was gonna help."

She bolted from the room, hopelessness and despair overwhelming her.

RUMOURS AND LIES

Maryn slammed her bedroom door and kicked her school bag across the room, wincing as her bare foot connected with the math textbook still inside it. She shook with frustration, fear, and guilt. Between leaving the kitchen table and slamming her bedroom door, she had made a decision.

"That's it, then," she said to herself as she hopped around on her good foot, rubbing her sore toes. "I've got to tell Mom and Dad—I've got to tell everyone—what I overheard in the bathroom." She was just about to go back downstairs to talk to her parents when her smartphone dinged. It was a text from Janey.

"heard something weird today r u there?"

"yes" Maryn texted back, her heart beat faster wondering if it might be something about the energy drinks.

"u & coach W"

"what?"

"that u r crushing on him"

"huh?"

"hrd it in the hall today & saw chatter about it 2nite"

"chatter? who?"

"everyone"

Maryn stared at the words on her screen and then jumped when her phone rang. She didn't even check who was calling. She answered it automatically, putting it to her ear as she said, "Janey?"

"Oh, hello, jock."

The tiny hairs on the back of Maryn's neck bristled. Stephanie.

"Have you heard the rumours?" her archenemy drawled. "About you and Coach Webber?"

"I don't know what you're talking about, psycho," Maryn replied through gritted teeth.

"Oh, well, you'll hear about it soon enough."

"Yeah, because that's what happens when you go behind our backs and tell your dad lies about us," said Julie. They had Maryn on speaker phone.

"I didn't tell my dad any lies about you. And I didn't tell him your secret either."

"Maybe not, but someone told the cops they heard us discussing the incident at school, and *you're* the only one that someone could be," Julie said. "It was supposed to be our little secret, remember?"

"We figure between your substance abuse problems and your recently outed love life, not to mention the *basics*...that even if you do go and blab on about what you think you heard in the bathroom, then nobody will believe you anyway," said Stephanie. "Not anymore, anyway."

"What do you mean, 'not to mention the basics?'" hissed Maryn. "What basics?"

"Oh, you know, that Julie and I both come from important families. My dad owns a really big high tech company, and Julie's mom runs the hospital; I'm the editor of the *Review*, and Julie and I are both on Student Council; and you're—well, you're the daughter of a dancer and a bike shop repair guy, and you hardly ever get your school assignments in on time."

Maryn fell silent.

"With everyone talking about this special relationship you've been having with your coach, who's gonna believe you if you say you heard us talking in the bathroom?" demanded Stephanie. "They'll just think you're trying to protect your boyfriend."

"You're *disgusting*!" Maryn yelled as she hung up. Someone tapped on her door. She sat on her bed, staring at her phone.

The tap came again, a bit louder this time.

"Maryn, may I come in?" her dad asked.

Maryn vibrated as if riding her bike over boulders. She cleared her throat. "Come in," she whispered.

"Are you okay?"

"No," she said. "Not okay."

Dad sighed and sat down on the edge of her bed, giving her space. "Maryn, you must feel a huge amount of frustration right now. And I can see that you're disappointed because we may not resolve this problem in time for the Provincial Championships. I really hope this whole incident with Coach Webber will be over soon, and that things will return to normal. But we have to accept that this is very serious.

When the wellbeing of two young people is at stake, the authorities simply cannot take any chances. And that's a good thing, really." He shifted a touch closer to her.

Maryn sat in the middle of her bed, knees to her chest, arms wrapped tightly around her shins. She rested her chin on top of her knees and stared into his eyes. He obviously hadn't overheard her yelling at Stephanie and Julie. He just thought she was still mad about their conversation at supper.

She wanted to tell him about the rumours. She wanted him to hug her and tell her that it would all be okay. But her face burned at the idea of telling him the kids at school believed she had a crush on Coach. Coach was Dad's best friend. The whole thing made her stomach turn, and she was certain her dad would be mortified.

"Dad?"

"Yes?"

"I've gotta get my head together to work on my history assignment. It's due next Tuesday. I'll be too busy this weekend with the race and the recital to get much done on it then. I've also got math homework for Mr. Churchill and an English assignment for Mr. Smith that's due next Wednesday. I handed in the outline for it today, but I'm still not really sure what I'm doing. I'm a bit lost."

"Is there anything I can do to help?"

"Just don't hack on me if you see my light on late tonight. I'm gonna bail on practicing piano, so at least I won't keep everybody up with my annoying repetitions."

"Okay," Dad said, giving her a light pat on the knee. "I'll leave you to get down to business."

He got up to go, but as he pushed her door open, Maryn said, "Dad?"

He looked back over his shoulder.

"I love you," she said.

He gave her a wink. "Love you, too, Sprint."

QUEEN BEES AND BFFS

"Janey?" Maryn typed, about two seconds after her dad left her room.

"yes" came Janey's immediate response.

"can u phone me?"

"yep"

The phone rang within seconds. "Janey?" Maryn asked.

"Are you okay?"

"No."

"Have you been reading the chatter?"

"What? No! I haven't been reading any of it."

"Good. It would only make you mad. And I think it's better for you to stay out of the conversation."

"Well, I'm not exactly *out* of it if I'm the main topic."

"Yeah, but you're not getting sucked in, and that's good."

"Have you gotten sucked in?"

"I've said my piece as your BFF, slamming them for talking trash."

"I don't know how I'll face everybody tomorrow." Maryn glanced at her race calendar. On the square for this Friday, she had written *PD Day*, meaning that Friday was a professional development day for the teachers. So at least she would have Friday off school and only tomorrow to walk among the haters.

"Well," Janey said. "Here's the deal. You show up and you act normal. *You* know it's all a lie. So that shouldn't be hard to do. People will see that Stephanie and Julie are pond scum."

"What makes you think people will believe us and not them?"

"It's because they're so transparent. Everybody knows how you kick their butts in sports without even trying. I think people are catching on that Julie and Stephanie just want to discredit your cycling talent. They're obviously jealous of you. I bet they imagined they would just breeze into the bike club and become the most popular girls there. Trouble is, they'd have to work hard for a long time to get respect. Their Queen Bee crowns aren't working for them with the Off-Roadies. Now they're embarrassed and they're making up stuff to distract people from how much they suck."

"Do you really believe that's what people think?"

"With a little help from your BFF...yeah. I even tweeted that they're hashtag-lame. And you know how much I hate writing hashtag anything!"

Maryn pictured the eyeroll that accompanied her friend's words. She smiled a little. "Thanks, Janey."

"You'd do the same for me."

Maryn snorted. "Janey, I've hardly had time to say two words to you this week. If this were happening to you, I might not even know about it!"

"That's true." Janey laughed.

"I suck at friendship."

"You sucked at friendship this week," Janey agreed. "But you're a great friend when it matters. Remember who stole my Hello Kitty lunch box back from Stephanie when she took it from my cubby in junior kindergarten?"

"Me."

"And who carried me on her shoulders underneath the school monkey bars so I'd feel like I could swing hand over hand like the other kids in grade three?"

"Me."

"Right. So forget about being a bad friend, and get your work done."

Maryn slumped back against the pillows and covered her eyes with her free arm. "How can I, when all I can think about is what people are saying about me?"

"Use some of that superhuman focusing ability your coach always has you guys working on. What would he tell you to do?"

"He'd say for me to take one important task at a time, zero in on it, stick with it, and get it done." Maryn sighed. "Then he'd tell me to move on to the next important thing. That's how he'd help keep me from getting overwhelmed. It's the same in races."

"See?"

"Oh, Janey." *Should I tell her? No, darn it! No, I can't.* Maryn squeezed her eyes shut. "Coach is, um...Coach is away. He had to go away right before my big race. It's just killing me."

"Wow," Janey said, quiet for a moment. "Maryn, I'm no jock, but isn't all the coaching he's done leading up to this race what matters? You know you're ready. You just have to put everything you learned from him into your race this weekend."

Maryn blinked up at the ceiling, considering Janey's words. "Whoa, you just schooled me in my own sport!"

"That's right. I rule. See ya tomorrow."

"See ya." Maryn sighed. She ended the call, then forced herself to turn off her phone so she wouldn't be tempted to check out the chatter. Then she regarded the pages spread out on her bed along with her books and laptop. It was getting late, and she felt like she'd just done the Hydro Line Loop towing a teammate or two behind her. There was no way she could pull an all-nighter to get everything done and still survive the next few days.

She reached over to her bedside table for her water bottle. The cool, familiar metal nestled in her hands. It was still at least a half full. But after a moment, she snapped the lid shut and pushed it away. Not this time. This time, she would work until eleven, and then quit for the night, because that's what Coach would want her to do.

I need sleep, not another boost.

WHISPERS AND GIGGLES

The smell of pancakes woke Maryn. Her mouth watered. Mmm, she bet her mom had made blueberry—her favourite. Maybe this day wouldn't be the disaster she expected it to be.

When Gil joined her at the breakfast bar looking alarmed and asking in a hushed tone if she was aware of the rumours about her and Coach, she managed a casual deflection. "It's just Stephanie and Julie and more of their grottiness," she said, as if heading to school to face a building full of gossipmongers was routine. "It'll blow over."

Her good cheer wavered a bit at school when people scrutinized her and girls giggled as she walked past them in the hallways. She tried turning Janey's assertion, "people know they're pond scum," into a mantra for herself. But it was tough to remember when boys in her classes raised their eyebrows, pointed and nudged one another.

In English class, Stephanie and Julie held court before Mr. Smith arrived. They whispered to a small group that had formed around their desks. Everyone seemed fully engrossed in what they were saying, and Maryn caught snippets of it, words like "creepy" and "pathetic." She ignored them, trying to concentrate on talking about the English essay with Janey. She was succeeding, too, until Joe suddenly tore across the room towards Stephanie and Julie.

"Are you *kidding* me?" he yelled at them. They just stared at him with expressions of bewildered innocence pasted on their faces.

"I don't believe we were talking to you," Stephanie said.

"We can *all* hear what you're saying, Stephanie. It's disgusting and it's made-up!"

"Well, obviously *you'd* stick up for your coach and his little pet," Julie scoffed.

"Stop talking. Both of you. You're out of your league this time, and you're smearing good people. Coach Webber and Maryn O'Brien are class acts, something neither of you would know anything about. So just shut up and stop making up this garbage. You're behaving like idiots."

Maryn and Janey both turned around in their seats, mouths and eyes wide open. Maryn had never known Joe to raise his voice or say a harsh word to anyone. Silence filled the room.

"Well, now this is a rare and wonderful occurrence," said Mr. Smith, who had just arrived. "Peace and quiet in the classroom? Could this be an intense interest in the writings of Edgar Allan Poe?"

***

Maryn, Janey, Omar, and Liam walked down the hallway between classes later that day. *This is becoming a thing*, Maryn thought.

"How's it goin'?" Omar asked.

Maryn made a face.

"Rough day?" Liam asked, wincing slightly. "Those girls are warped."

His words made her feel a bit better, but she didn't respond.

Omar pointed at the book Janey carried, *The Female Man*. "So that's, like, feminist sci-fi, right?"

"Yeah, I'm not so sure about the feminist sci-fi thing," Janey said. "I'm kinda working my way through the classics right now. How 'bout you?"

Maryn wanted to keep moving and get out of the crowded hall, but she also welcomed the shift in focus. She pretended to search for something in her bag while Omar and Janey compared reading lists.

"I'm reading *The Stand*, you know, Stephen King?" Omar continued. "Apocalyptic stuff...killer virus. But I plan to read *The Hitchhiker's Guide to the Galaxy* next, to lighten things up."

Liam, who was waiting for Omar, fiddled with somebody's locker padlock. They were standing in the corridor outside the science lab, nowhere near their own lockers.

"Do *you* read science fiction?" he asked Maryn.

She peeked over her bag and shook her head. "Not at all! Never. No."

He chuckled at the forcefulness of her response. "Me neither."

"Sounds like we're both stuck in the 70s," Janey said to Omar, and then blushed and stood mutely. She glanced over at Maryn as if hoping for her to talk.

Maryn frowned. Why did Janey suddenly seem so awkward with Omar? They'd known him forever. And Janey usually couldn't stop herself once she started talking about science fiction novels!

A crush of students jostled them as the bell sounded. For a few seconds, the four of them stood together in a protective little circle that reminded Maryn of how she felt in her sanctuary. Soon, however, they drifted apart as the boys went one way and the girls another. Class was about to begin.

***

As the day went on, Maryn paid less and less attention to the whispers and giggles. Her spirits even lifted during history class when Ms. Price gave them the entire period to devote to the assignment. Once Maryn got going, she completed a large portion of her project, boosting her confidence that she could in fact get it done by the due date next week.

"Janey," she said at lunch. "You know how I've been using energy drops to give me a boost for, like, months?"

"Yes, despite multiple warnings from your BFF."

"My mother hen, you mean."

"Ha ha."

"Yeah. Well, last night I chose sleep over my energy drink, and I woke up able to think more clearly. I mean, I do feel a little sluggish right now. Maybe that's caffeine withdrawal. But even so, I had a breakthrough with the sonata this morning."

"Wow."

"Then I had a great breakfast and knew I could come to school and act normal like you said."

"Cool."

"Then Joe stuck up for Coach and me and it was so...so..."

"Awesome?"

"Yeah. Like a boost of high-test energy drops!" Maryn laughed. "And then I dug in during history class and got a bunch of work done on my assignment, and that gave me a boost too. As my dad would say, I think I may have been barking up the wrong tree this entire time."

"Wow. That's huge."

"I know! I think I had to feel the change starting in my body to believe it. Some of my jumpy, grouchy, stressed-out feelings over the past few months may have actually been fueled by this stuff. Why didn't I see it?"

"Better late than never, right?"

"Right."

They both focused on their meals again, and for a few minutes they ate in a comfortable silence against the chaotic background noise of the cafeteria.

"Hey, Janey?" Maryn finally asked.

"Yes?" Janey gathered up her lunch litter, getting ready to return to class.

"What's the deal with you and Omar?"

"Me and Omar? What are you talking about?"

"Earlier today...you guys seemed, well, different."

Janey raised an eyebrow. "Different how?"

"Well, um, awkward and maybe shy. Do you like him?"

"Of course I like him."

"No, I mean do you *like* him, like him?"

"Give it up, Maryn, seriously. Omar and me?" Janey stood up abruptly, her face turning pink. "We're both sci-fi nerds. That's all. Get it?"

Maryn blinked at her friend, suspecting otherwise, but not daring to say so. She nodded. "Got it."

"Good."

Janey stomped away.

CALM AFTER THE STORM

On Friday, the PD day, all four of the O'Briens grabbed breakfast in the kitchen, getting in each others' way as they prepared to go in several different directions. Mom was running a dance camp at the studio, Gil was doing an extra training session with his baseball team, and Dad was taking Maryn to the race site for a practice ride.

"Hey, Maryn, did you get that history assignment done, or did you get an extension?" Gil enquired.

"I don't need an extension for every project I'm assigned!" Maryn gave her brother a look that would peel the hard finish off a weather-proof paint job. Her lift in spirits of yesterday had dropped like a stone. She'd woken up with a headache, upset that it was Friday and Coach Webber was still under investigation. And now Gil was checking up on her school work? She scowled at him.

"Ms. Price gave everybody a full period to work on it at school yesterday," she informed her brother in a waspish tone, "so I should be able to get it done by next Tuesday, which is when it's *due*. Would you like me to report back to you on any of my other subjects?"

"Nope," Gil said, his expression going tight. "Excuse me for breathing."

Remorse tugged at Maryn. *Darn! Why am I so horrible to him?*

"Today's ride will kick-start your race visualization, Maryn," Dad said.

A wave of self-pity washed away the remorse, and Maryn's scowl returned. "You're *not* my coach, Dad."

"That's *enough*, Maryn!" Mom said.

"Darby, it's okay," Dad said, putting his hand on her shoulder. "Maryn's tired and probably a bit overwhelmed. There's a lot going on for her right now."

"Don't talk about me like I'm not here!" Maryn yelled. "A *bit* overwhelmed? Try freaking out. The Provincial Championships are on Sunday and Coach isn't back. *Why* isn't he back? He didn't do anything. How could they possibly need more than a couple of days to figure that out?"

Before anyone could react, Maryn thundered out of the kitchen and out the front door. There, not knowing which way to turn, she threw herself down on the front steps, the storm inside of her conflicting with the bright sunny morning. She was still there when Dad found her a few minutes later.

"I know this is tough," he said, sitting down beside her. "But it's not right to take it out on the rest of us."

"I get it. I'm out of control. I know you all think I'm tense all the time, but I've never been *this* stressed and angry before. Sometimes

I'm so mad I can hardly breathe."

"Well, let's try to channel some of that energy into your racing, okay?"

"I'm sorry, Dad. You're a good coach. I know that."

"Well, Coach Webber really is something special, so it's hard for me to compete with him. We're just gonna have to make do with what we've got right now."

Maryn smiled at her dad, trying to show her appreciation.

"Let's get going," he said, patting her on the back.

***

"Okay, Sprint," Dad said, swinging his leg over his bike and settling onto the seat. "Let's hit the trail and see what kind of ride you have to look forward to on Sunday."

Maryn mounted her bike and pushed off, taking the lead. One benefit to living so close to the race venue was that they could familiarize themselves with the trails without having to travel far. Her dad and Charlie would lead some practice rides for the entire team on Saturday, but this PD day ride would be a father and daughter run-through. She was happy they had the trails to themselves.

"You can take this washboard section at almost full speed." Dad's voice vibrated on the hard ripples of the soil trail behind her. "It'll be a rough ride, but you can handle it. The next hill's a bit of a grinder, but long uphill climbs are your forte. This is where you can put some serious distance between you and the others."

His familiarity with the small ski resort from his years of mountain biking in the area gave her dad a bit of an inside scoop. It was a challenging course for the Ontario Cup circuit, and a good choice for the Provincial Championships, but weather conditions could change the trail surfaces and foliage along the way, and grooming or adding man-made features such as bridges could alter the trails. So it would still be critical to scout the course today.

Maryn couldn't help grinning. As good as it felt to be out on the course today, it was even better to be out there with her dad. He was so passionate about the sport. And he had such confidence in her. She *did* feel strong spinning up the long hill. She was ready. She'd been training hard, and she was in top form.

"You can put the hammer down on the other side of this hill. It's a scream. But watch out because I recall it being deceptively steep. Try to get into the zone in this next section, but don't zone out. Do you know what I mean?"

"Yup. Get a good strong cadence going, but pay attention."

"That's right. Ride fast and ride hard, but keep your eyes wide open."

Dad had gone out ahead during their descent, and he'd turned the corner ahead of her. As Maryn rounded the corner herself, he ducked to avoid some branches. The trail had narrowed significantly. "There's a vegetable tunnel here!" he yelled.

"Good to know, Dad." Maryn laughed at the leaves stuck in his helmet from the unintentional pruning he'd done on the foliage.

They stopped at the top of the course's longest and steepest hill to take a drink and survey the forest and river below. "I'm glad we rode the course, Dad. It's technical, and it's helpful to know about the really challenging sections in advance. Surprises are *so* not cool in an important race."

"Agreed. But just remember...you're trained to handle every rogue branch, puddle or rock that crops up out there. You're also naturally good at responding in the moment."

Maryn nodded. "Thanks, Dad. I'm ready to prove to Coach that I can be an Olympian—that I'm ready for the next step."

"I know you are, Sprint." Dad downed the last of his water, pushed the spout closed with the heel of his hand, and then clipped his shoe into his right pedal. "Ready?"

"*Way* ready."

***

Maryn rose early on Saturday morning to practice piano and get a start on her English essay. She also nearly completed her work on the history assignment. In the afternoon, she went to race registration with her dad.

Her headache persisted. *Could this be withdrawal from the energy drops?* Her gut clenched at the thought. Then again at the realization that Emma Sutcliffe had arrived at the race site.

Registration opened at three. She and her dad had been there since two fifteen. They had opted to register as early as possible so her dad could get out and ride with the team before the trails became clogged with like-minded competitors. Maryn busied herself with kneeling down to mess with her chain derailleur, but contact with her rival was inevitable, so after a couple of minutes she stood up again. Hands on hips, she gazed purposefully over at Emma, giving the girl a respectful nod.

Emma smiled and waved back. "Hey, Maryn! How was your drive?"

"Short." Maryn smiled.

"Oh yeah, you live pretty close by, right? I forgot about that."

"How was your drive?" Maryn scanned the area for her dad and spotted him chatting with one of the race officials.

"It was great! Smooth sailing, cool tunes, sunroof open..." Emma broke off when a bunch of her own teammates swarmed her. They hugged one another and patted each other on the back as if they'd been apart for years. It was annoying to watch. Everyone seemed so pumped, perky and puffed up with confidence. Maryn was a bit embarrassed to be standing in the line-up alone. So it was perfect timing when her smartphone vibrated with a text from Janey.

"wassup?" Janey's message said.

Maryn leaned her bike against her hip to free up her hands. She texted back, *"in line for registration"*

"what next?"

"ride the course with the team. you riding Buddy today?"

"ya! 2 days in a row—gotta love pd days! Btw, I'll be at the race"

"r u sure? races stress you out"

"I told u as bff I can't miss your big race + it's close to home"

"u r the best. r u coming for supper tonight?"

"yep c u then"

"c u"

Maryn watched Emma and her friends while the volunteers examined her bike. She had to admit Emma seemed like a really cool girl—somebody she might actually be friends with if the other girl wasn't already her archrival. She searched the crowd for Brooklyn Morrison, who would be another contender for Provincial Champion in their category, but there was no sign of her yet.

Maryn sighed and went back to watching the volunteers and waiting for her own teammates to arrive.

***

Later that evening, after a lively and delicious pasta supper with her family, Janey, and Zoe, Maryn lay in her bed, riding every bit of the course over and over in her mind's eye. By the time she finished, she knew all its sharp turns, undulations, and narrows; its sudden temperature shifts; the heat that hit as she broke out into the open meadows with their tall grasses and buzzing insects; and the cool that came as she passed under the cover of pine trees where soft needles formed slippery cushions in the scented shade. She drifted off to sleep feeling she knew the trail like an old friend.

TAKING THE LEAD

The next morning, unseasonable warmth greeted the bikers as they assembled near the start of the race, making Maryn feel as if she'd come down with a fever.

"Since when is it this hot at eight thirty in the morning in September?" she groaned, wiping away the sweat already dripping from the end of her nose. She armed her bike cages with bottles of water minus the energy drops.

"It is definitely a scorcher," her dad said as he mopped perspiration from his own brow. "But don't worry, Sprint. Think back to your long hours of training in the blazing heat of the summer. This won't bother you a bit." He smiled, putting his arm around his daughter and briefly squeezing her to him.

"You're right." She nodded her head. "I've done the heat training to handle this. Thanks, Dad."

Emma Sutcliffe approached with her coach and posse. They were a noisy bunch, using voices many decibels louder than the muted tones she and her dad had been using.

"You've got this Emma!" one tall teenaged boy bellowed.

"You *so* do!" A girl chimed in, holding up a sign that read 'Sutcliffe Rules!' and adding, "This race is yours!"

Maryn turned her back on them, closed her eyes, and took a deep breath. She so wished Coach was here for her today. She could use the kind of support Emma was getting. She blinked back a haze of tears and scowled at herself. This was no time for a pity party—she had a race to ride. Glancing at her parents, brother, and Janey, she smiled. *They* were here for her. Her dad smiled back and gave her a thumbs-up.

Her mom came over, hugged her warmly, looked her in the eye, and said, "Have a really great race, Maryn. We'll be here cheering for you, from start to finish."

Gil, who had followed Mom over, put his hand on Maryn's shoulder. "Race like you mean it, sis."

Janey waved nervously from a spot on the fence line. She always said she didn't like to interfere.

Maryn clipped together the buckle of her helmet strap as a small group of younger Radical Off-Roadies ran over to wish her well. The more experienced riders were either busy preparing for their own races, or already out on the course.

"You can do it, Maryn!" encouraged Melissa.

"Yeah! Go really, really fast," said Priya.

Maryn grinned at them. "Thanks, girls!"

The announcer called Maryn's age group to the start line. Her heart pumped hard and her hands shook as she gripped her handlebars and got into position, but this time, it was just nerves, not energy-drop agitation. She had the experience to know she could channel all of her nervous energy, excitement and anticipation into an explosive start. She located both Emma and Brooklyn before getting into position.

When the starting pistol cracked, Maryn broke out ahead of the pack, letting the others know she meant business. She was easily the first cyclist to enter the forest trail where the course narrowed, about a hundred metres from the start. Within another minute or two, she found a good, strong rhythm in both peddling and breathing. Her own breaths and the crunch of gravel beneath her wheels filled her ears.

She tackled the course aggressively, taking each turn as planned and each straightaway with strong, confident pedal strokes. She checked for Emma and Brooklyn as she powered across one of the open meadow stretches. Her archrival sprinted in hot pursuit just twenty metres back. *That's okay,* Maryn thought. *Seeing you there just makes me want this more.* There was no sign of Brooklyn yet.

She geared down and increased her cadence to spin up the long, gradual climb where her dad had said she would put serious distance on the others. *Answer this!* she silently challenged Emma, climbing hard, fast, and away from her rival and then 'putting the hammer down' just like Dad told her to on the steep downhill that followed.

The racers in Maryn's age group had to complete the loop three times. She felt capable and in control as she passed her supporters on the first loop. Janey stood clapping by the fence, and everybody else's positive cheers gave her a boost.

"Go! Go! Go!" yelled the little girls.

"Way to stick to the plan, Maryn!" shouted her dad.

"Looking good, Maryn, looking strong!" called her mom.

"Stay tough!" hollered Gil as she re-entered the woods.

She kept up the intensity on the next loop, despite the ever-present burn in her quads and the morning's oppressive heat. But as she passed the crowd for the second time, a wave of discomfort passed through her body. Emma's supporters called out, "She went out too fast! She's dying. You're closing the gap!"

Maryn glanced back to see if Emma had started gaining on her. It didn't seem like it, but she increased her cadence anyway. *Only one loop to go*, she reminded herself as the heat enveloped her like a suffocating cloak. The words of Emma's friends ricocheted through her mind: "*She went out too fast!*"

But what had her own supporters said? She concentrated hard, conjuring up the image of them stationed at the edge of the course, her dad clapping, whistling, and looking calm; her mom smiling with assurance; Janey biting her nails; the girls still screaming *"Go! Go! Go!"* and Gil running alongside her for a moment or two. *"Don't listen to them Maryn, you know what you can do!"*

Her thighs stung as if they'd been set ablaze beneath her skin, and her stomach protested against an agonizing queasiness. Maryn began to wonder if Emma's supporters were right. Had she gone out too fast? She hadn't trained in this kind of heat for weeks!

Why is the negative stuff always easier to believe? Maryn thought. *Come on. This is yours. You can do it. Don't let a bit of pain get in the way of proving to Coach that you're ready for the Canada Cup circuit. You can take it. It's just a few more minutes!*

She increased her cadence even though her heart rate was climbing out of control. *Just another two-thirds of a loop,* she told herself. She turned again to look for Emma and was shocked to see her just ten metres behind.

Come on, Maryn! Get going. Push. Push!

CRASH COURSE

As Maryn negotiated another sharp corner, she looked for Emma again just as her front wheel hit the washboard section of the trail. Startled to see Emma now just a bike length away, she was even more startled by the bumps of hard soil. She spun back to focus on what she was doing, but it was too late. She lost her grip as her tires jittered madly across the uneven surface, and the bike slid sideways. She overcorrected and bounced off course, lunging into the thick brush at a treacherous pace. Suddenly, her front wheel hit a monster chunk of rock and the bike stopped dead in its tracks, catapulting her into the trees at the same blistering speed she'd just been peddling. She landed hard, pain shooting through her entire body. She couldn't tell where it came from. Couldn't move. Couldn't breathe.

She stayed still for a moment, getting her bearings. Slowly, things began to register through the shock. Her bike lay on its side by the boulder she'd hit, wheels spinning in silence. Rocks and sticks poked into her back. Warm liquid trickle down the back of her neck and over her shoulder. And a voice called her name.

"Maryn? Maryn! Where are you? Are you okay? Answer me so I can find you!"

Emma Sutcliffe.

Maryn took an experimental breath. It hurt, but not too much. Emma called again.

"Over here!" Maryn responded faintly. "I'm over here."

Emma arrived in an instant, dropping her bike beside Maryn's. "I couldn't see you because of these bushes," she said. "Oh, you're bleeding!" She knelt beside Maryn and gently cleared away twigs and ferns so she could get to Maryn's shoulder.

"Emma." Maryn tried to push her away. "You should be racing. You can win this. I'm okay—just go!"

"I'm not leaving you."

"Go. Go! We had a huge lead on the rest of the pack. You can still win this!"

Emma ignored her. "Are you hurt anywhere else? Do you think you've broken anything?" she asked.

Maryn struggled to sit up.

"Be careful!" Emma warned, supporting her back and examining her head. "It looks like you're bleeding behind your ear. I think this might have stabbed you when you hit the ground." She held up what appeared to be a sharp stick, its end glistening red, then surveyed the wound again. "Hold still, it's bleeding a lot."

Emma pulled off her jersey, reached over for one of her water bottles, then soaked the fabric and began using it to clean the blood from behind Maryn's ear to get a better look at the wound.

"Well, it looks horrible, but it's not life threatening." Emma pressed the wet jersey against the cut to try to stop the flow.

"Emma. I'm so sorry!" Maryn was now certain she was okay. She had moved her arms and legs and turned her head. Aside from scratches, bruises, and being stabbed by a stick, she figured she was fine. "You could have won. You could have sent somebody back for me in a few minutes."

"Don't be crazy, Maryn. I couldn't keep racing without knowing if you were dead or alive."

"But I told you I was okay. I told you to go."

"Hey, some things are more important than winning. You would have done the same for me." Emma smiled, putting more pressure on Maryn's wound and patting her on the back with her free hand.

Maryn searched her archrival's blue-grey eyes for any sign of sarcasm, but only saw sincerity. Emma was right. Suddenly, as if someone had held up a lens to the world for her, everything came into focus. Coach Webber, Stephanie, Julie...all of it. And she knew what she had to do. She could hardly wait to do it. Why had it taken a serious crash for her to see it?

ACTION PLAN

Maryn's family, Janey, and Maryn's teammates ran towards her, their expressions registering various levels of terror and worry as Emma helped her along. The pair had just emerged from the opening to the forest trail, each pushing their own bikes.

"I broke Rocky, Dad," Maryn said as they reached her.

"How are *you*? Are *you* broken?" her dad asked, taking Emma's place and putting his arm around his daughter's waist.

"I've got Rocky," Gil said, seizing the Rockhopper from his sister. Everybody else crowded around the two girls, anxiously firing questions at them and then listening in rapt silence to the story of Maryn's accident as well as Emma's kindness and clever first aid. All the while, Maryn's head swirled with plans.

The St. John's Ambulance staff, volunteers who provided first aid for race events, confirmed she would need stitches to close the cut behind her ear. Before leaving for the hospital, Maryn and her parents hugged Emma, and both she and Emma sought out Brooklyn to congratulate her on becoming the Provincial Champion.

"It's not how I wanted to win," Brooklyn admitted. "You both raced great. I would've been third."

"You never know," said Maryn. She gave Brooklyn an encouraging smile. "I feel really bad for Emma, though."

"Let it go, Maryn," Emma said, shaking her head but smiling too. "I made my own decision out there, and it was the right one. Here's to a fresh start next season!" She took a swig from her water bottle, and Maryn and Brooklyn joined her by clinking water bottles and then taking drinks from their own.

It was almost noon when the O'Briens and Janey left the race site for the hospital. They opted to take Maryn to one of the small town hospitals close to the ski resort. They were happy to be in and out—with Maryn checked over and stitched up—within an hour.

***

Once Maryn had cooked up an action plan, she pushed ahead with it. Her injuries didn't slow her down, they infuriated her. Fortunately, fury energized Maryn.

During their drive home from the hospital, she told her family every last detail about what had happened over the past week, including the conversation she had overheard in the bathroom at school, her use of energy drops on school property and at home, and all of Stephanie and Julie's threats and lies—both in-person and online. Once Maryn started telling her story, her dad pulled the truck over so he and her mom could turn in their seats to give her their undivided attention.

Her dad shouted in disbelief about the seriousness of teen-aged girls "toying with a good man's life," then became even more incensed by the rumours about his daughter having a romantic relationship with Coach Webber.

"I feel sick," he said when Maryn had finished. Mom offered to drive the rest of the way home. When they got out of the car to switch places, they embraced one another at the side of the road for so long that Maryn, Gil, and Janey all looked away to give them some privacy.

When her parents climbed back inside the truck, Dad asked Mom, "You're *sure* you're okay to drive?"

"I'm fine," Mom said. "I'm numb. This'll all sink in later for me. But I think Maryn's right. We need to deal with this swiftly." She gave Dad's face a gentle, lingering pat, then thrust the truck into gear and stepped on the gas.

WHEELS IN MOTION

"What are you thinking?" Maryn whispered to Gil as they drove. He'd been staring out the window in silence while their parents talked in low murmurs in the front seat.

After what seemed like ages, Gil spoke. "I punched a guy for saying that stuff about you and Coach," he said.

Maryn eyeballed him, shocked. "Whoa. Did you get in trouble?"

"Kinda," he said. "I was at practice. Mr. Hyatt sent me home to cool off. He said he'd talk to Mom and Dad about it after your race weekend."

"Sorry," Maryn said. "And, um, thanks."

Gil gave his sister a grin and then went back to watching out the window. Maryn turned her attention to Janey.

"I'm so sorry I couldn't tell you everything about what was going on," she said.

"I understand," Janey said. "But I don't really get why you believed that Coach Webber would kick you off the team for taking those drops. They aren't illegal or anything."

"I guess I was more worried about him thinking I couldn't handle everything. You know how much I want the Canada Cup thing—I think I was afraid he might hold me back because of it."

Janey nodded, and then, like Gil, they both fell silent and stared out at the passing world.

* * *

"Maryn, it's Sunday afternoon," Dad said when they arrived home. "I'm sure most people have already made plans. Why don't we try to organize an emergency board meeting for tomorrow night, instead?"

"Dad! That's the thing about emergencies...they can't wait. *I* can't wait. *Coach* shouldn't have to wait. Please, Dad, please just see how many of these people you can pull together?" Maryn implored. Her scratches and bruises made her look like she'd been mauled by a wild cat. Her dad exchanged looks with her mom, and then led the way to his computer to locate everyone's contact information.

"I really wanted to sleep on this before we faced those girls and their parents in person," he said, reaching for the phone on his desk, "but I understand the urgency and I'll do everything I can to make this happen today."

He started making calls.

The key players on Maryn's list—compiled along with her parents—were Ms. Topping, the Principal of Maryn's school; Stephanie Harwood and her parents; Julie Davis and her parents; Quentin Dorian, the bike club manager; Pia Bianchi, the bike club board president; and Maryn's parents. Dad reached everyone. The Harwoods initially requested a conference call rather than an in-person meeting, but they agreed to attend a meeting that evening, provided "the accused" would not be present.

Principal Topping arranged for the meeting to take place at the school, the most neutral location. Mom explained to Maryn that, even though the allegations against Coach were the more important issue, it was still important to be fair.

"Principal Topping also needs to know about the energy drops on school property," she said. "And about the bullying that's been taking place on her watch, and *online* by her students."

Maryn trembled a little at the thought of being the one to share these revelations. She had decided to tell the truth about everything that had happened over the past week. She no longer feared being accused of lying. She no longer feared the consequences. Coach Webber deserved this. He'd deserved it one very long week ago, but she couldn't change that now. Despite her new resolve, however, she still feared speaking in front of Stephanie, Julie, and a room full of adults.

But the meeting was her idea, and the wheels were in motion now.

GOING THE DISTANCE

"Hey! Doesn't your recital start at four o'clock?" Janey asked. "That's in forty-five minutes."

Maryn and Janey worked together in the O'Brien rec room, preparing for the meeting later that evening. Janey was helping Maryn gather digital evidence of Stephanie and Julie bullying her.

Maryn looked at the clock and sighed. "My parents think I'm crazy to perform today. They want me to call Mrs. Landers to explain about my accident."

"So are ya gonna give it a miss?"

Maryn hesitated, then shook her head. "No. Mrs. Landers is counting on me being there. And besides, when I think about how much work I did to get ready for it, I feel like I should do it, you know?"

"Why do I get the feeling you'd be there even if you had both hands in plaster?" Janey asked, chuckling.

"Ha! That may be true. I better get changed and start walking. It'll take me a few minutes to shuffle down the street to St. Andrew's."

"I'll be your escort."

"It's nice of you to offer, but I know how much you love going out to the barn on Sunday afternoons."

"Are you kidding me?" Janey exclaimed. "This day just keeps getting better and better. I'm in it for the long haul."

***

"I thought you hated these recitals," Gil said, walking alongside his injured sister, Janey, and his parents on the way to St. Andrew's Church.

"Well, it may be my last one for a while," Maryn said. "Mom, Dad, and I talked about it this afternoon, and we all agreed that if I plan to train and race mountain bikes at this level, it would be better if I just play piano for fun from now on."

"For *fun?*" Gil said, making a face.

"Yeah, without the exams, festivals or recitals. Just, you know, play."

"Will your teacher be O.K. with that?" Gil asked.

"Yes. She's been hinting at if for a couple of years now. But I've been ignoring her. I thought I could keep doing it all. Mom and Dad pointed out that if I have to take energy drinks to stay awake long enough to practice, then something might not be right."

"Will you still have to take lessons?"

"I don't have to. But I want to. It'll still be good to have Mrs. Landers' help with new music."

"So today may be your last recital *ever*," he said.

"Yeah," Maryn said, shuffling along the sidewalk behind her parents.

She blinked back unexpected tears at the idea. "I guess maybe you're right."

***

"Break a leg!" Janey, Gil, Dad, and Mom all called out together, as if they were part of a chorus. Maryn's face warmed, but so did her heart. It was good to have their support here, too. She headed off to join the other piano students on the pews at the front of the church.

As she sat in the vaulted, dimly-lit space, waiting for her turn to play, Maryn studied the spacious room filled with the parents, siblings, grandparents, aunts, uncles, and friends of Mrs. Landers' many students. She'd been performing at recitals in this church since she was five, but no matter how prepared she may have been for any of them, she always experienced a nervous flutter in her stomach as she waited for her turn to play. Her hands got sweaty every time too. Her mom said those were signs that she cared about the quality of her performance. And she did...just maybe not as much as she cared about racing.

Thinking of her mom, she glanced back at her people and impulsively gave them a little wave for old time's sake, just as she would have done when she was in kindergarten. Her mom winked back.

Just like old times.

When it was her turn to play, she rose and walked up the plush carpet of the stairs to the familiar old Heintzman baby grand piano on the raised dais. She took her time adjusting the bench to exactly where she needed it to be, breathed deeply, and she was off.

As her hands flew over the keys just like her wheels had flown over the rocks, twigs, and leaves earlier that day, she let a part of her mind wander, thinking about how much all those years of recitals had taught her about herself. Between them, Mrs. Landers and Coach had helped shape the person she had become. The person who was going to pay back Coach tonight by telling the truth. Maryn couldn't help but smile at the idea, and then she pulled her attention back to the present, knowing that Coach would want her to focus on her piece right now rather than letting her mind wander. Mrs. Landers may have taught her how to tackle the challenging pieces, but it was actually Coach who had given her the mental skills to master them when it mattered most.

Just this morning, she had lost her focus in her race with disastrous results. She had no intention of making the same mistake this afternoon. She zeroed in on what she was doing, giving it her all. As she got closer to the section she'd been struggling with, she forced herself to relax and believe. *You've done the work. You've got this,* she reminded herself. And then...she went for it.

At near-virtuoso speed, she played every note in the run with confidence and clarity. She felt more alert and alive than ever before while performing piano. In her mind, Coach's voice urged her to "go the distance," reminding her that her race wasn't over quite yet and that she needed to concentrate until she crossed the finish line.

The echoes from her final notes faded away, and she tingled in the hush that followed. She peeked at her family, at Janey, and at Mrs. Landers, in awe of what she had just experienced, and then let out an involuntary whoop of joy that brought down the house when everyone erupted into an easy bout of laughter.

TRUTH BE TOLD

At 8:00 p.m., Maryn rose to face the assembled group. This was it. The moment of truth. *Her* moment of truth. She wiped her palms against her jeans and swallowed hard against the paralyzing fear that gripped her throat. She could do this. She *needed* to do this—and not just for Coach's sake. She opened her mouth to speak, but before she could utter a word, Stephanie shoved back her chair and stood.

"We're not staying if *she's* talking," she blustered, beckoning to Julie. "We came because we believed there had been a development in the case. We thought the police had called this meeting to update us." She glared at her co-conspirator and whispered fiercely, "Come *on*, Julie. What are you waiting for?"

Julie scanned the adults sitting in the room. She half stood, but scowls from both her parents made her rethink, and she lowered herself into the chair again. Fighting her own desire to flee, Maryn blinked in surprise when Stephanie's mother took her daughter's arm and pulled her back down in her chair.

"Stephanie, what on *earth* has come over you?" Mrs. Harwood exclaimed. "My apologies, Maryn, please carry on." She hissed something else into her daughter's ear when Stephanie tried to speak.

Seeing Stephanie scolded in front of everyone helped restore Maryn's courage. She planted her feet firmly on the floor, cleared her throat, and proceeded to tell her story. She didn't stop talking until she had said everything she wanted to say. She looked people directly in the eye as she spoke, at first taking comfort from the encouraging eyes of her parents, then moving to the bike club officials and Principal Topping. She ended by looking straight into the eyes of all the Harwoods and Davies.

At first, Stephanie and Julie shook their heads and folded their arms, as if Maryn talked nonsense. But Maryn had done her homework. With Janey's help, she had compiled some facts about Stephanie and Julie's bullying of her. She hadn't kept a diary, but she was able to recollect and write down the different ways in which Stephanie and Julie had threatened her, and Janey had printed out the entire online conversation thread in which Stephanie and Julie had spread the rumours about Maryn and Coach Webber.

As Maryn presented the evidence, Julie's gaze dropped, then her head drooped, then her shoulders slumped. Stephanie, on the other hand, kept her nose in the air and her arms folded. She rolled her eyes and continued to behave as though Maryn's words were ridiculous lies.

"I feel responsible for what happened to Coach Webber this week," Maryn said, her eyes stinging and her voice cracking. She paused to swallow and clear her throat. "I was so busy protecting myself that I didn't stand up for him and tell the truth when it really mattered. I understand now that I could have shut down this whole thing right away. But I was scared. I kept hoping it would all go away on its own. And when Stephanie and Julie spread lies about me having a crush on Coach Webber and said people would think I was just protecting my 'boyfriend' if I told the truth, I believed them!"

Julie's parents looked at one another as if thunderstruck. Stephanie's parents both fixed icy glares on their daughter. She shifted in her seat and glared menacingly at Maryn, but this time, Maryn met her gaze without flinching.

"I was afraid of being suspended," she continued, lifting her chin and squaring her shoulders. "And I was afraid that if Coach Webber found out that I was taking energy drops to get through, he wouldn't allow me to advance to the Canada Cup circuit. But I was *wrong* to be afraid, because none of that matters. Nothing is more important than a person's reputation, his job and...well, his life."

The silence in the room that followed reminded Maryn of the silence in the forest right after her crash. She held her breath, wondering what would happen next—terrified to find out what the damage would be. But this time, she hadn't lost focus and crashed. She had kept her focus, held her head high, faced both her supporters and her enemies...and was now prepared to face the consequences.

CONSEQUENCES

"Okay so *that* was the longest day of my life so far. I'm just *whipped!*" Maryn exclaimed, as she talked with Janey on the phone the next morning. Her parents had given her permission to stay home to recover from the crash and from the meeting. She was lying in her bed, going over the previous evening's events with Janey. "Thanks again for helping me find and print out all that online bullying stuff yesterday."

"No problem," Janey said. "I was happy to help, and it was an added bonus that I got to cause a hot mess for Stephanie and Julie."

"Yeah," Maryn said. "It seemed like they were in a lot of trouble when I left the school last night. Ouch!" she yelped as she shifted on her bed, trying to get comfortable. "Everything hurts. Seriously, I feel like I was hit by an eighteen wheeler or trampled by a pack of...a pack of... pachyderms," she said. She tried not to laugh because it hurt too much.

"I think most pachyderms come in *herds* not *packs*."

"*Really?* You're giving me an English lesson when I'm in agony over here?"

"Well, it was more of a biology lesson, or, more specifically, ethology—the study of animal behaviour."

"Right." Maryn treated her best friend to a pointed silence.

***

On Wednesday after school, Principal Topping called Maryn, her mom, and her dad in for a meeting in her office. She told them that she, the police officer, Coach Webber, and the two key board officials had dealt with Stephanie and Julie on Monday and Tuesday.

"Since the entire incident was so carefully contained, Coach Webber opted not to press charges against the girls," explained Principal Topping. "He feels that his reputation—and the reputation of the bike club—remains intact because of how the investigation was handled."

She pursed her lips, looking stern as she continued, "The girls narrowly avoided being charged with public mischief. The police have recommended, and their parents have agreed, that the girls make recompense to their community by doing fifty hours each of community service. In addition, the bike club has revoked their memberships, and I've suspended both of them for two weeks for engaging in bullying. Stephanie has also lost her position as editor of the *Review,* and both girls have been removed from Student Council."

Principal Topping turned her attention to Maryn, and her expression softened a bit as she went on to explain that, although she greatly admired Maryn's courage in coming forward with her revelations, it was part of her job, as principal, to see that school rules were respected.

"Unfortunately, Maryn," she said, placing her warm hand on Maryn's shoulder as she delivered the news, "It is also my job to ensure that there are consequences for those who break our rules."

She explained she would be giving Maryn the minimum one-day suspension for having the banned energy drops on school property, mainly because Maryn had expressed such deep remorse for her actions.

"I suggest you take the suspension day tomorrow," Principal Topping said. "I, for one, would like us to move forward from these unfortunate incidents as expeditiously as possible."

FULL SUSPENSION

Maryn sat in the warm sun on the O'Brien's front porch steps in her sock feet and pajamas. It was eight forty-five on Thursday morning. Half awake and ready to serve her one-day suspension, she picked absent mindedly at the bits of grey paint peeling off the well-trodden entranceway as she waited to say goodbye to her dad before he left for work. She'd already missed her mom, who had left for the dance studio, and Gil, who had left for school.

She rubbed her bleary eyes. Just then came the unmistakably familiar hum of a particular mountain bike, spinning up the driveway. It skidded to a stop, just centimetres from where she was sitting.

"Coach!" Maryn cried, jumping to her feet and catching the drawstrings of her baggy boxers to prevent them from dropping to her ankles.

"Maryn, you pajama-sporting hooky player!" Coach Webber straddled his bike and smiled, a merry glint in his eye.

"I'm not playing hooky, I got suspended." Maryn laughed. It was wonderful to stand in front of Coach again. She'd imagined this moment for days, but she'd pictured a gloomy encounter with tears, apologies and disappointment. And here she was, laughing! Shame washed over her, and she swallowed, her smile fading.

"Coach, I messed up, I..."

Coach Webber put up his hand to stop her from continuing. "Maryn! I don't want to hear another word about how you 'messed up.' You're nothing but a great kid, a dedicated athlete and a loyal friend."

She held his gaze for a brief moment until a clatter from the side of the house drew her attention. Dad? And not dad dressed for work, but fully outfitted in his mountain biking gear. Maryn blinked at him as he pushed his bike over to her and Coach Webber, threw one hand in the air, and exclaimed, "What's with the PJs, Sprint? We're hittin' the hills today."

Her gaze travelled between him and Coach. "What?"

"That's right, "Coach Webber said. "With this awesome weather and the whole day in front of us, we had no choice!" He winked at his best friend.

"But Dad has his shop..."

"Closed!" shouted her dad, slapping his handlebars for effect.

"But I'm suspended!" she said, giving them both a look that said, *are you guys for real?*

"There's no better suspension than full bicycle suspension!" Her dad chuckled, pushing down hard on his handlebars and bouncing the bike up and down to demonstrate.

"Dad, you can't be serious."

"I *am*. And I'm jacked for a great day of single-track riding with my daughter and my best friend. We're just wondering why you're still in those pajamas."

***

As they rode along flat open terrain in the beginning minutes of their ride to get Maryn's still-sore muscles loosened up, Coach and Maryn discussed the next season of mountain bike racing.

"I already knew you were ready to join the Canada Cup circuit next season, Maryn," he said.

Her jaw dropped and her bike skewed sideways. She straightened it out.

"And your struggle with high school, piano, the energy drops, bullying, and my investigation only served to reinforce what I already believed: that you are *absolutely* ready," Coach continued comfortably.

"But how is that possible?" Maryn shook her head. "I took the drops to get through."

"Yes, but you also figured out that your way of handling things wasn't sustainable, and you adapted. You asked for help when you needed it. You adjusted your workload for a more balanced situation next season. You learned a lot. You found your own solutions to some pretty serious problems. You should be impressed with yourself."

Saplings whipped at Maryn, and her legs burned as she pushed a challenging pace that kept her just behind Coach and slightly ahead of her father. Her eyes were wet and salty, but with sweat and not tears this time. She breathed in the tangy scent of the trail and its rotting leaves, slippery mosses and turned-over earth, and felt like she was filling up with something immense and immeasurable.

"What is it?" Coach shouted, looking back at Maryn as he made what her dad would call a 'gnarly' turn on a steep incline.

"It's everything! Everything is good," Maryn called back, giving him a wide smile. Then she put the hammer down and powered up the hill just like one of the guys.

Because everything wasn't just good, it was *great*.

ACKNOWLEDGEMENTS

I would like to thank a few key people for their help seeing me through this book: my wise editors Jennifer Latham and Linda Poitevin; my savvy designer Jen Hamilton; my dedicated adult readers Donna McCloskey, Ruth Browning, and Jennifer Shepherd; my honest young guides North, Sydney, Keili, and Zane; and my patient and infinitely supportive husband Andy.

ABOUT THE COVER ARTIST

JOCELYN VAN WYNSBERGHE

Inspired by the Canadian wilderness, Jocelyn compresses
the enormity of nature into her attic apartment and pulls
colourful landscapes and funky book covers from imagination
accompanied by her cat Ace.

Her paintings are all "oil on canvas."

Made in the USA
Columbia, SC
23 October 2017